He closed the distance ▮▮▮▮▮▮▮▮▮▮▮▮▮▮▮▮ barely a breath of air s▮▮▮▮▮▮▮▮▮▮ look like you have everything under control right now." His voice was deep and husky.

She could step away. She could change the subject. She could do a hundred things to head off what was coming next.

She did none of them.

His hand came up to cup her jaw and Livia leaned into the touch. Oh, how she had missed him. His thumb drifted over her lips, and she parted them, wanting to taste him, to know him again.

"*Almost* everything under control," he said, his voice a dark growl, then he leaned in and kissed her.

His mouth didn't just meet hers—it caressed hers. Lips drifting slowly over hers at first, tasting, relearning, exploring. She yielded to him, opening her mouth, curving into his kiss, his touch.

Livia pulled away, and broke off the kiss. Her body ached in protest. "We…we can't do that," she said. "We're not…together anymore." The two words sounded harsh and cold.

She stepped back again, and cradled Piper—*his daughter*—closer to her chest. This was what was important. This was what would last. This was what needed her attention, her full focus. Her child. Not the man who had broken her heart.

Dear Reader,

Welcome back to Riverbend! I love this fictional little town in Indiana, and after several books set in the town, I'm starting to feel like Earl and Betsy live next door to me. I started the Riverbend stories with *Miracle on Christmas Eve,* then continued it with *Marry-Me Christmas* and then revisited the town again in *Midnight Kiss, New Year Wish.* I truly love writing about this town each year, and love writing these holiday books while I'm celebrating the holidays in my own house.

In *Family Christmas in Riverbend,* the Christmas tree lot that first appeared in *Miracle on Christmas Eve* becomes a predominant element in the plot. I think that's because I'm a sucker for Christmas trees. I put mine up as soon as we clear the Thanksgiving table, and love finding new ways to decorate the tree. When my kids were little, we'd lie under the branches and peer up at the lights, watching them twinkle above our heads. It seemed so magical, like a nighttime sky right in the living room.

I hope you enjoy *Family Christmas in Riverbend,* and I hope you love the residents of this little Midwestern town as much as I do. Like many of my characters, I love to cook during the holidays, so be sure to check out my blog, www.shirleyjump.blogspot.com, to see what's cooking in my kitchen or visit my website, www.shirleyjump.com, to see what's next for my books. You can also write to me at P.O. Box 5126, Fort Wayne, IN 46895.

I hope your holiday season is magical and special, and that Santa brings you lots of books!

Shirley Jump

SHIRLEY JUMP
Family Christmas in Riverbend

™
Harlequin®

TORONTO NEW YORK LONDON
AMSTERDAM PARIS SYDNEY HAMBURG
STOCKHOLM ATHENS TOKYO MILAN MADRID
PRAGUE WARSAW BUDAPEST AUCKLAND

Recycling programs
for this product may
not exist in your area.

ISBN-13: 978-0-373-17771-4

FAMILY CHRISTMAS IN RIVERBEND

First North American Publication 2011

New York Times bestselling author **Shirley Jump** didn't have the willpower to diet, nor the talent to master under-eye concealer, so she bowed out of a career in television and opted instead for a career where she could be paid to eat at her desk—writing. At first, seeking revenge on her children for their grocery-store tantrums, she sold embarrassing essays about them to anthologies. However, it wasn't enough to feed her growing addiction to writing. So she turned to the world of romance novels, where messes are (usually) cleaned up before The End. In the worlds Shirley gets to create and control, the children listen to their parents, the husbands always remember holidays and the housework is magically done by elves. Though she's thrilled to see her books in stores around the world, Shirley mostly writes because it gives her an excuse to avoid cleaning the toilets and helps feed her shoe habit. To learn more, visit her website at www.shirleyjump.com.

Books by Shirley Jump

HOW TO LASSO A COWBOY
MIDNIGHT KISSES, NEW YEAR WISHES

Other titles by this author available in ebook

To my husband and my children—who have made every Christmas a magical, wonderful time of year. There is no gift more precious to me than hugging and kissing all of you on Christmas morning.

CHAPTER ONE

PEACE. Quiet. Tranquility.

That was what Olivia Perkins had been picturing when she'd returned to Riverbend, Indiana, at the beginning of December. For the past year, Livia had thought of Riverbend often, missing the calm she had found in the little Indiana town in a way she'd never missed anything before.

A native New Yorker, Livia had always considered herself a city girl. Until she'd spent three amazing, wonderful weeks in Riverbend last New Year's Eve, helping her boss Jenna plan a birthday party. And now, she'd gone and done it.

Moved here.

She'd bought a little house on a quiet side street, loaded all her possessions into the back of a U-Haul, secured Piper in her car seat, then driven out here and settled in—just in time for her first Christmas in the sleepy little town. She'd bought a tree from the Methodist Church's lot—after a long, chatty conversation with Earl Klein, who took a personal interest in every tree and customer. He'd helped her tie it to her car and waved off the bills she tried to hand him as a tip. As soon as Livia got home, she'd set the tree up in her front room, before she'd finished unpacking the stack of boxes in the kitchen.

Now Livia stood in that very kitchen and watched across the street as the neighbors draped strings of multicolored lights over a trio of thick, squat shrubs. It was the perfect complement to the herd of lighted reindeer on the right side of their lawn and the blinking wreath adorning their front door. Nearly every house on this street had the same Christmas touch, a neighborhood medley of red and green.

Livia sighed. It was all so…perfect. Like images on a holiday postcard. She wished she'd moved here earlier. In time to see the trick-or-treaters dashing up and down driveways, or the straw bales stacked on lawns for Thanksgiving.

She'd definitely lingered too long in New York. Understandable, she supposed. Change wasn't something she'd been very good at. At least not until a bright fall day in September that turned Livia's life upside down. In a good way.

Livia smiled at the thought of her three-month-old daughter, asleep just down the hall in the nursery. Amazing how one little baby could transform a grown woman's life. The moment she'd held her newborn daughter in her arms, Livia realized there was no other place on earth she wanted to raise her child but in Riverbend. The town had the perfect blend of hokey charm and Midwestern values that would wrap around Piper like a thick blanket.

She could just imagine Piper riding a bicycle down the town's quiet side streets while the neighbors waved and shouted a how-ya-doin'. She could see herself taking Piper downtown on Saturday afternoons for an ice cream cone where Mr. Duval would undoubtedly overindulge his youngest customer. Livia was already anticipating the delight in Piper's face the first time she saw the rainbow of Christmas lights at the annual Riverbend Winterfest and heard Santa's hearty ho-ho-ho.

Yes, Riverbend was perfect for raising a child. For beginning a family, even if it was a family of just two.

Livia exited the kitchen and headed down to the nursery, her hips swaying in time to the beat of the Christmas music spilling from the stereo's speakers, adding a Norman Rockwell air to the house. Piper slept soundly, her tiny chest rising and falling with each whispered breath. God, she was a beautiful baby. A wave of gratitude and love washed over Livia.

Piper had changed Livia's life in a hundred ways—a hundred wonderful ways. Never for a second did she regret the choice to raise her child alone. She'd do it better, she vowed, better than her own father had, and certainly better than her absent mother. Livia would make sure Piper never knew that painful hole of losing a parent. But even as Livia made that silent promise, a part of her whispered doubt.

Was she really saving Piper pain? Would Piper miss what she had never had or known?

Livia tiptoed out of the nursery and tugged the door shut. At the top of the stairs, she paused and thought of the man who had unknowingly blessed her with Piper.

Edward Graham.

The owner of a nationwide chain of event venues, including the now closed Riverbend Banquet Hall, Edward had swept her off her feet when she'd been here last year and whisked her into one of those heady, unforgettable romances. When she'd finally come up for air, she'd realized the one thing their whirlwind relationship had been missing—substance. Edward was all about the charm, less about the long term.

She should have known something that started so fast would end up in flames. Edward had been a handsome but mysterious and private man who had let her into his bed but never fully into his heart. Like a fool, she'd hoped for more and stayed in Riverbend that winter for another week, waiting for him, before she finally realized he'd meant it when he'd said he was done with her, with their relationship, with the town. That he was never going to be marriage material, or anything even close to that. She'd returned to New York and buried herself in her work, running the New York branch of Jenna Pearson's party planning company.

Until she saw a tiny plus sign in the window of the pregnancy test.

That day, she'd thought of calling Edward, then stopped herself. Livia had heard through the grapevine that Edward had come back to town only long enough to sell his house, pack up his car and leave Riverbend for good. Without a word to her or to anyone else.

What had she expected, after the way they'd ended things? Still, it had hurt.

Not a little. A lot.

Now here she was again, in the town that had changed her in so many ways. Livia walked through the house, straightening this, arranging that.

Everything was perfect, exactly the way she liked it. The house was clean and neat, the decorations hung just so. The little house practically gleamed, as shiny as the gold star atop the tree that stood patiently in the corner, waiting for Piper's first Christmas. A half-dozen gifts for Piper sat under the branches, but Livia didn't need or want anything. She had Piper. And—

The front door flew open. "I hate this place!" A slam punctuated the sentence. The door shuddered in its hinges.

And Melody.

Livia shot a glance at the baby monitor on the counter, but there was nothing more than the whisper of air coming across the airwaves. Her heavy sleeper daughter hadn't stirred. Phew. "Why do you do that? You could have woken up the baby."

"Sorry." Melody dumped her coat and bag on the floor, then toed off her boots and kicked them aside. "I had a *really* bad day. You know how worked up I get when things go wrong."

"Yes I do." Too well. Livia retrieved Melody's things from the floor, giving her sister a hint-hint wave, which Melody ignored. Livia lined the shoes up by the door, put Melody's bag on the counter, and hung her coat up in the closet before returning to the kitchen.

Melody plopped into one of the kitchen chairs with a dramatic sigh. "I don't know why you thought living in this godforsaken town was a good idea. If I'd known this place didn't even have a Starbucks, for Pete's sake, I never would have come to visit."

So much for peace, quiet and tranquility. None of the three were words that she associated with her little sister. Who had, for some insane reason, decided to follow Livia to Riverbend. An afternoon visit had turned into an overnight stay, and was now verging on a permanent relocation.

"If you hate it so much, why do you stay?" Livia asked.

Melody crossed her arms over her chest and pouted. "Because I'm not going back to Boston until Carl gets a clue."

Carl, Melody's fiancé, who it turned out, had been engaged to, and pledging his eternal love to, a woman named Jackie at the same time. That hadn't gone over well with Melody, who had thrown a suitcase in her car and driven straight to Livia's new house. Livia had been tempted to give her sister a lecture about her tendency to choose every Mr. Wrong on the planet, but Melody had been crying so hard, Livia didn't have the heart. Instead, she made up the spare bed and ordered a large double-cheese pizza.

She'd figured Melody would cry for a couple days, then do what she always did—go back to the city, to her friends, her busy life and to yet another man. Instead, she'd stayed. And stayed. And stayed.

And complained nearly every single minute.

"Maybe you should look for a job," Livia said. "I'm sure it'll help take your mind off things. There's probably plenty of people in need of an interior decorator in this area."

Melody huffed. "*Home stager,* not interior decorator. They're two entirely different things."

Livia bit her lip. "Either way, I'm sure you could—"

"My car broke down right in the center of town," Melody interrupted. "I swear, this place hates me. Good thing that Earl guy was there. He towed it to his shop and gave me a ride home. I bet it's broken forever. It was making this whining noise and—"

"I'm sorry to interrupt, Melody, but I need to run an errand." Truth was, Livia had no interest in hearing the latest drama in Melody's life. There'd been the eyeliner meltdown first thing this morning, the stuck waffle in the toaster at breakfast and the too-small sweater in the dryer. And that was all before ten.

Livia grabbed her coat, flung her scarf around her

neck, then swiped her car keys off the table. "Can you stay? Piper should nap for another hour. If she gets up, just call me. You don't have to do anything."

"That's because you don't trust me."

"I do."

Melody arched a brow.

"Okay, maybe not entirely. But Piper's just a baby and you're…"

"The irresponsible little sister." Melody sighed. "I have grown up, you know."

"I really have to get to the store before dinner. Can we talk about this later?"

"Where are you going?" Melody's face lifted in hope. "Are you going somewhere fun? Can I come?"

"Just the grocery store. For, uh, milk and stuff." And whatever number of purchases could give Livia a few minutes of peace. Shopping alone was about the only way she'd get some. She loved her sister but Melody had a way of making every little thing into a BIG DEAL, complete with capital letters, wild gesticulating and over the top shouting. "You know how you hate grocery shopping. Besides, you promised you'd help out more and staying here while Piper sleeps is helping. Because you are living here for free, remember?"

Melody detoured for the sofa. She reached for the remote and flicked on the TV. "Okay, fine. But get me some chocolate milk, will you? And cookies. Oh, and chips, and some of those pizza bite things. You don't have anything good to eat around here."

"Because that stuff isn't good for you. If you'd just—"

Melody put up a hand to cut off Livia's argument. "Spare me the no-sugar life lecture. Geesh, Livia, you need to lighten up a little. Look at this place. You could eat off the floor. All five servings of vegetables and your whole grains, of course." She swiveled around to face her sister. A bright cascade of light from the television danced across her features. "A little fun won't kill you, you know."

"I gotta go. I'm not debating what I put in the cupboards or how often the house needs vacuumed. Again." Livia turned and headed out the door.

Winter had yet to breathe its snowy kiss over Riverbend. The air held a promise of snow, but over the last few days, there'd been nothing but one quick icy rainstorm. The cold world around her looked gray and bleak, not quite the postcard image of the holidays she'd had last year when she'd been here.

Livia drove the few blocks from her house to the main street of Riverbend. Melody's words ran through her mind. Yes, Livia liked things clean. And with a baby, it was doubly important to keep the environment organized, clean and healthy. Why couldn't Melody understand that?

Either way, Livia refused to let it get to her. Instead, she let the Christmas spirit filling Riverbend wash over her. Even without snow, it was a holiday oasis. What the town called "downtown" didn't even compare to a New York City block, but Livia loved it all the same. Small charming stores, all hung with Christmas wreaths and bright red bows, and friendly residents who had remembered her from last year and greeted her at every turn. Despite the gloomy weather, the town had Christmas cheer in abundance.

She parked in the side lot of the corner grocery store and headed inside. The electric-eye door whooshed shut behind her.

"Nice to see you again, Miss Perkins!" Cal, the store manager, sent her a quick wave.

"Thanks, Cal. How's business?"

"Busy as heck, thank the Lord. Seems everyone and their uncle is here in town for the holidays." Cal swung his wide frame out from behind the customer service counter. "How are things for you?"

"Just fine, just fine."

"Glad to hear it." A customer stepped up to the counter, so Cal sent her another wave and went back to work.

Livia grabbed a cart and started down the first aisle. She greeted Betsy Williams and Earl Klein, two lifelong Riverbend residents who'd been instant friends when she moved here. Most of the town was like that—friendly and warm.

No wonder Jenna had chosen to settle here after she'd married Stockton Grisham, her childhood sweetheart and owner of the elegant Rustica restaurant. Once the holidays were over, Livia would go to work for Jenna, part-time at first. Once she'd moved to Riverbend, Jenna had switched her event planning business focus from birthdays and weddings to charitable events, and had found fulfillment and happiness that Livia could hear in her voice. That was the kind of life Livia wanted, the kind of example she wanted to set for her daughter.

She wandered the aisles of the Sav-A-Lot. Livia hadn't really needed a thing at the store—except for an escape from Melody, and a moment of peace, a bit of time to herself, something she hadn't had in months. Christmas carols played on the sound system, and before long, Livia found herself singing along. Her spirits lifted, and the stress of Melody's stay abated. She loved her sister, she really did, but living with her—that was a whole other ball of wax.

She'd forgotten how difficult her little sister could be. Their mother had left when Melody was only six and

Livia ten. Melody had been far more affected by that than Livia, and had never really taken to Livia stepping into the mother hen role. There were days when Livia wished she'd been able to just be a kid, but their father had been working nonstop, and someone had to be in charge. Maybe it had been a mistake, but Livia had done the best she could.

Livia paused by a display of sparkling wine, her hips swaying in time to "Jingle Bell Rock."

"If I remember right, you were a Reisling girl."

The deep voice came from over her right shoulder, but she didn't need to turn to see who had spoken.

Edward.

Livia froze and willed herself to be cold as ice, but a shiver of heat ran through her all the same. Her heart raced, and the parts of her that refused to listen to common sense rang with awareness. *Edward.*

She swallowed hard, and wished the memories of her heart could overpower the memories of her body. Images flashed through her mind unbidden—his hands running over her body, his lips drifting down her neck, his voice, hot and low, whispering in her ear—but she pushed them away, cemented them behind the wall she'd put in place nearly a year ago.

She was done with him. D-O-N-E.

Finally, Livia turned. "Edward. I didn't realize you were in town."

"Just got in this morning. And the fridge is empty, so…" he held up a half-filled grocery basket, "here I am."

He was back? For how long? Didn't he wonder why she was here in town?

She told herself she didn't care, nor need to know, the answer to any of those questions. That it didn't affect her at all to see his piercing blue eyes. That she didn't want to reach up and push back the errant lock of dark brown hair that skimmed across his brows. That her gaze didn't drift to his mouth and wonder if he'd still taste as good now as he had then.

Edward.

She turned away, grabbed the first bottle of wine she saw and stood it in her cart. Even though she didn't need it, and probably wouldn't drink it. It was merely a prop, a means of escape. "Well, I'll let you get back to your shopping." She started to take a step.

Then he spoke again, and her body betrayed her once more. *"Livia."*

When he said her name like that, the memories rushed back in a wave, tumbling and tossing in her mind, breaking past her mental barriers. The steamy nights she'd spent in his arms, the playful mornings she'd spent in his bed, and then—

The heart-wrenching end.

The realization that their relationship had been something deep and meaningful to her—and not to him. That she'd been nothing more than a holiday—

Fling.

In the hundreds of moments since she'd wanted to pick up the phone and share the news about the baby. But every time, she had stopped. Before her fingers could dial, she remembered those last moments, the ones that had shattered all those silly schoolgirl emotions that Edward had awakened in her.

Damn, damn, damn. Why did he have to come back? At Christmas, of all times? She shook her head, willing him to go away. "I'm sorry, but I've got to—"

"Don't go," he said at the same time. He reached for her, but his hand fell short, and a whisper of cool air danced over her fingers. "Stay. Just for a second. Let's catch up, over some coffee or something."

"I don't think that's a good idea."

He offered her the lopsided grin that had haunted her nights for months after she'd returned to New York. "For old times? 'Auld Lang Syne' and all that?"

"That's for New Year's, Edward. It's Christmas. Ask me again in a few days."

"And will your answer change then?"

She shook her head, and something akin to a knife sliced through her heart. She thought of Piper, asleep in her crib back in the little house on Elm Street, completely unaware that her father wanted nothing to do with her. She thought of telling Edward about Piper, but stopped herself. She already knew his reaction. He didn't want their baby then, and he wouldn't now.

"No, it won't," she said. "We're done, and that's not going to change."

This time, Livia did walk away and headed down another aisle, before her common sense could be overruled again. And she fell for the only man who had ever truly broken her heart.

The log split with a sharp crack, the two halves landing on the ground with twin thuds. With the back of his hand, Edward swiped the beading sweat off his brow, then reached for another log. He swung the heavy axe up and over his head, then forward, watching the arrowed blade slice into the maple.

The pile of chopped wood beside him grew by another two chunks and the air held the sweet, earthy scent of fresh-cut logs, but the frustration in his chest had yet to subside. He laid the axe on its head, then dropped onto an overturned stump and took a breath.

Livia.

He'd heard she'd left Riverbend shortly before he had. He'd never expected that she'd return, much less settle down in the town.

Hell, he hadn't expected *he* would return. And he wouldn't have, if it had been his choice. Particularly not during the holidays. He'd been perfectly content to stay in his Chicago office, managing the remaining properties in his portfolio while he waited for a buyer for the company, and retreating to his apartment at the end of the day for a glass of bourbon and mindless television. Then the hospital had called, saying his father had had a heart attack, and Edward had gotten on the first plane back to Indiana. During his father's hospital stay, Edward had flitted back and forth between Riverbend and Chicago, and when Ray was finally ready to come home, Edward had put his company in the hands of his vice president and moved into his father's house. Truth be told, he hadn't been doing much of the day-to-day work before he handed it over. All that had done was make it official that Edward was no longer helming Graham Venues. Now here he was, chopping wood to stoke a fire that would keep his father warm.

"You're a stubborn man."

Edward turned and shot his father a grin. "Who do I think I learned it from?"

Raymond Graham scowled. "I told you I could chop my own wood. I'm not dead, you know."

True, but the heartiness had dimmed in Ray's features. He'd lost twenty pounds—something his already lean frame couldn't afford—and he seemed to have gained twenty years in his face. "Dad, you just had a massive heart attack—"

"One that would have killed a lesser man."

"Exactly my point. And that means you shouldn't be chopping wood or, hell, even standing out here in the cold." If anything could have pulled Edward out of his self-created prison, his father's illness was it. He'd stay long enough to get Ray back on his feet, to make sure his father was fully healed, then head somewhere else. Maybe somewhere warm.

Didn't matter as long as it was far from Riverbend and the mistakes that haunted him at every corner. Once upon a time, he'd thought he could be happy here.

He'd been wrong.

He wasn't the kind of man who settled down, had a couple kids and painted the porch on the weekends. He didn't know much about himself, but he knew that.

"Damn doctors," Ray said. "Always putting rules on me."

Edward looked at his father askance.

"All right, all right. I'll go back inside and bundle up under the blankets like a big baby. I'll even take a nap if it'll keep you from harping on me. I swear, you're worse than the nurses."

Edward grinned. "Call it payback, Dad, for all the lectures I got as a kid."

Ray waved off the words. "You ask me, you deserved them. You were always off in your own world. As distracted as a bee on the first day of spring. Biggest daydreamer I ever met."

Edward scoffed. "And look where it got me. I should have listened to you and gone to work at the factory."

His father let out a long breath that frosted in the cold air. "You did the best you could."

"It wasn't enough." Edward jerked off the stump, grabbed a pile of wood and started toward the house. But his mind wasn't on the woodpile or even what had happened in this town last winter. It was on another winter, long in the past. In his bank account, he had millions, but it didn't matter. No amount of money bought peace. Or forgiveness. "It wasn't nearly enough."

"That girl didn't get hurt because of you. It was an accident. You keep blaming yourself for things you can't control, son."

The words sliced through Edward, as cleanly as the axe had slid through the wood. He froze, the cold, hard logs clutched to his chest. He could see Miranda Willett's face, her bright eager eyes the first day she came to work. He'd hired her, but hadn't known the nineteen-year-old very well. In their short interview, she'd talked about working at the hall to save money for college. Apparently she'd gotten early acceptance to one that offered the perfect graphic design degree program she wanted, but even with scholarships, the school was out of the financial reach of her parents. He'd half heard her, thinking she was nice and earnest and good enough for the server position he was filling. A few minutes later, Edward had retreated to his office, buried himself in paperwork. The hall manager handled the employees, and the day-to-day. Edward had been telling himself for months that he should spend more time on the floor, getting to know the people who worked for him. And now, when it came to a nineteen-year-old server named Miranda, it was too late. She'd been so young—too young to get hurt like that. If only—

He'd tread the path of If Only a thousand times and it never erased the past. Or the horrific fire that had destroyed Miranda's life.

Or the mistakes Edward had made long before Miranda Willett was even born. Mistakes that should have taught him he was better off alone. Mistakes that reminded him every day why he had no call planning a future with a woman like Livia. No matter how much he craved it.

"I should have never come back here," Edward said, the words icing in the cold air. "I can't change anything."

Then he headed into the house and stoked the fire, warming his father's house but not his own heart. That had gone cold last January when the place he had built his dreams upon went up in smoke. Taking an innocent person's future with it.

CHAPTER TWO

WHEN Livia got home from the store, she spent a long time standing in the nursery she'd created in the tiny third bedroom of the house, really more of a glorified closet than a room, marveling at the miracle of her daughter.

Edward's daughter.

The beautiful child they'd created together—a child he'd made it very, very clear, he'd never want.

"He's the one missing out," Livia whispered to her daughter. Piper's tiny chest rose and fell beneath the pink fleece sleeper, her delicate hand curled into a tight ball. A dusting of blond hair whispered up and down with the slight breeze from the ceiling fan above, the one noise that seemed to lull Piper to sleep.

"Oh, Piper, if only he knew what a gift you are." She ran a finger down the silky softness of Piper's cheek.

Piper stirred, and opened her eyes. Big blue orbs took in the room, as if it were the first time she'd seen the space. Her gaze drifted over the cartoon zoo that decorated her bedding, then up the crib rails, until finally, locking on her mother's familiar face. Her three-month-old features lit with joy and she started to squirm, her hands and arms reaching. Livia reached down and curled her daughter into a tight embrace. She inhaled the soft strawberry scent of her skin, then pressed a kiss to Piper's cheek. Her heart swelled to bursting with love and gratitude for this place, for her life, and most of all, for her perfect minifamily of two. "Hey there, beetle."

Piper opened her mouth, and let out a half scream, half cry. Moment of peace over. Livia laughed. "Okay, okay, let's get right to the food."

She carried Piper back to the kitchen, then heated a bottle and slipped it into Piper's mouth. The baby sucked greedily, her cheeks hollowing with each slurp.

Livia looked down at her daughter and though Piper had light hair, she had her father's features, too. His eyes, the slight dimple in his left cheek, and most of all, his smile. For the hundredth time, she wondered if she should just show up on his doorstep with Piper.

I never want children, Livia. Never. I don't need that kind of albatross around my neck.

His last words to her, thrown at her in their final argument, had rung in Livia's ears for months. Every time she thought about telling him about Piper, she heard those words again. And kept her sweet daughter to herself. Rather than see Piper hurt by her father's rejection. Livia knew too well how a parent's indifference could hurt.

Once Piper was fed, Livia sat her in a bouncy seat while she put the groceries away, then set to work making some chicken and rice soup. She could have opened a can, or even served last night's leftover spaghetti and sauce, but instead she took the time to poach fresh chicken, throwing onions, garlic and spices into the water, then dice up carrots and celery.

Seeing Edward again had turned her inside out. She refused to think about him, to wonder how he was. To wonder if he had changed. Instead, she stayed busy in the kitchen. That was far better than daydreaming about a man who didn't want the same life she did. Cooking relaxed her, brought her back to ground. And so she cooked.

A half hour later, the kitchen smelled like heaven and steam from the simmering pot glazed the nearby windows. Livia mixed up a quick biscuit dough and plopped the doughy circles into the oven.

Melody came to stand in the kitchen, resting her head against the doorjamb. She eyed the pot with a dreamy, soft expression, then drew in a long inhale. An air of vulnerability, of openness, hung on Melody's delicate features. "Chicken and rice soup? Didn't Mom used to make that all the time?"

Livia nodded. "I'm surprised you remember."

"Yeah, me, too." Then the moment of vulnerability was gone before it even started. Melody stepped into the kitchen and gave Piper a quick kiss on the head. "Hey there, you smelly monkey."

"She hates being called that, you know."

"Then how come she just smiled at me?" Melody bent down to Piper and beeped her button nose. "'Cause you're a monkey, that's why."

Livia laughed. "You're a terrible aunt."

"Too bad, because I'm the only aunt she's got." Melody came to stand beside the stove. She picked up a spoon, dipped it into the soup and slurped up a taste. "Mmm. It tastes just like Mom's."

"It's from her recipe."

"Really?" Either the steam or the memory made Melody's eyes glisten, and Livia felt an echoing ache in her own heart for the mother they'd barely known before she'd walked out on her husband and children.

"Where'd you find it? I thought Dad got rid of every-thing."

Their father had done a massive purge of the house in the weeks after his wife left. It was as if he thought tossing boxes out the door would assuage his grief over the betrayal. It hadn't done anything but leave the house bare and lifeless, and made it seem as if their mother was a mere whisper of a memory, not a vibrant woman who had left them as quickly as a summer rainstorm.

It had been especially hard on Melody, who had fewer memories and mementos than Livia. What none of them had was answers, and it seemed all Livia had done for the past seventeen years was to try and cover up that gap in information and relationship.

Their father had bought a pair of big puffy chairs and a huge, ugly kitchen table to fill the space, but it wasn't the same. Maybe she could talk her father into visiting for Christmas. It would be good for all of them to get together. Still, a part of Livia doubted it would happen. Even when she'd lived in the same city as her father, he'd always been too busy for more than a quick hello. Either way, that was a mountain to climb another day.

"Before I moved, I stopped by Dad's house and while I was there, I went up to the attic," Livia said to Melody. "I guess I never really thought about whether there might be stuff up there, especially all these years later."

"Was there much?" Melody fiddled with the spoon, as if she could care less about the answer.

They rarely talked about their mother. Livia wondered sometimes if it was because Melody didn't like to be reminded of all the memories she'd lost. "There wasn't a whole lot," Livia said. "Mostly boxes filled with old Christmas decorations and our baby clothes. But in one of them, I found her cookbooks and her recipes."

Melody took another sip of soup. "I'm glad you did."

The moment of détente extended between them, and for a moment, Livia had hope that she and her sister could finally have the kind of bond other sisters had. As the protective oldest, Livia had never felt they were like other siblings. She'd been too worried about making sure Melody ate three meals and did well in school to do anything else, such as form a connection over checkers. Melody, with her loud music and dramatic moods, was the total opposite to Livia's quieter self. Piper had been a bridge for the two, but not enough.

Melody tossed the spoon. It landed with a clatter in the sink. "So, who's this Edward guy?"

Livia hadn't thought a few simple words could so radically change the mood in a room, but those words did it. She went from nostalgic warm fuzzies to frosty detachment in a second. "No one."

"That's not what I heard." Melody sing-songed the words. "Word about town is that you two used to date. I can't believe you broke up with him, sis. He is *yummy*."

"How do you know what he looks like?"

"He's in the paper today." Melody waved a copy of the *Riverbend News* at Livia. "Front page and everything."

"It's a small town. A dead deer on the road gets front page treatment." But still Livia took the paper from Melody and dropped into a kitchen chair to read the article.

Edward's smiling face stared back at her. It was an old photo, the one he'd used for publicity for the banquet hall. She knew the current look—a little messier, a soft layer of stubble across his jaw, and thicker, longer hair. But the eyes—the eyes were the same. A vibrant blue, so deep it seemed like she could drown in those eyes.

She jerked her attention away from his face and over to a small but conspicuous headline: Local Millionaire Back In Town?

The article was mainly speculation. Some gossip had noticed Edward's return and wondered if he'd come back to rebuild the banquet hall or just for a family holiday visit.

The building may not be smoldering any longer, but whispers about the tragic accident at Riverbend Banquet Hall last year are still in the air. Has Edward Graham returned to try again? Does he think Riverbend has forgotten what happened there? Forgotten how Miranda Willett suffered in the days since? The suddenly silent Graham didn't return repeated calls for comment.

Livia's heart panged. Edward didn't deserve that kind of vicious speculation. That fire hadn't been his fault. Yes, it had had a terrible consequence. She remembered reading the articles about Miranda's brush with death and her difficult months of recovery. The fire department had cleared Edward of all responsibility, noting he hadn't even been on the premises when the fire occurred.

She remembered that day clearly. She and Edward had gotten together for lunch, with a promise to see each other on Saturday. He'd gone back to the hall to get some work done before knocking off early to get some rest after a particularly hectic week.

The sirens had awakened Livia. The next morning, she'd seen what the fire trucks had been rushing to save. What she hadn't seen was Edward. They'd talked only once in the days after the fire—one long, heated argument that told her everything she thought about Edward was a lie. And that it was over between them.

She'd been living a dream, and that day had brought her screeching back into reality. Edward hadn't wanted her comfort, her advice, or anything else from her. He'd shoved her away, and that had been it.

Nevertheless, the Edward Graham she knew was never irresponsible. Never blasé about his business or the safety of his employees. It seemed no one else believed that, though. For a second, she thought of calling the reporter and telling her she had it all wrong.

Instead, Livia put the paper down.

Edward could—and probably would—fight his own battles. Except, he hadn't this time, which wasn't like the Edward she knew and remembered. Since his return, he'd apparently kept a very low profile. What happened to the ambitious business owner she used to know?

"I don't care what he's up to," Livia said to Melody and to herself. She crossed to the stove to check the soup. The rice was done, so she reached for the shredded, cooked chicken and began dropping it into the broth.

"*Sure* you don't." Melody grinned, then sobered. "Wait…if I do the math…is he…is Piper…?"

Livia sighed. "He's Piper's father."

"Wow. And he doesn't know?" Livia shook her head. Melody let out a low whistle. "Well, that explains a few things."

"Explains what?"

"Like why you were talking to him today at the supermarket."

Livia paused in adding the chicken. "How do you know that?"

"Livia, this town is smaller than a postage stamp.

Someone burps and there's a phone tree to alert the neighbors."

Livia shook her head. Melody had that right. "Betsy called you?"

"Nope. Earl. He stopped by to drop off my car. It's all fixed now. A broken fan belt, he said. Man, am I relieved. If it had been something bigger, I don't know how I would have afforded to pay the bill. That car is just a pain in the…"

Livia wasn't listening. Darn that Earl. He was one of the nicest people in Riverbend, but he had a tendency to play matchmaker. She should have known, after seeing him and Betsy—his lady friend, as he called her—in the market, that they'd say something. And of course, they had. Darn small towns.

Melody rattled on about her car. Livia ladled some soup into bowls, then placed them on the table and grabbed the biscuits from the oven. She sat down across from Livia and slathered butter all over until the biscuit glistened. Livia waved off the butter and tore off a piece of biscuit to dip into the soup. Piper sat between them, watching their meal. But Livia's mind wasn't on her dinner—it was on the article about Edward. Had he returned for good?

And if so, what was she going to do when he found out about Piper? In a town this small, it was inevitable.

"So, are you going to tell him?" Melody asked, as if she had read Livia's mind.

"I don't know." Livia sighed. "I just don't know."

"Don't you think he has a right to know?"

"Yes, but…"

"But what?"

Livia paused for a long moment. "But I don't want him hurting Piper, like…"

"Like Mom hurt us." Melody finished the sentence, the decades-old betrayal fresh in her eyes.

Livia nodded. "Yes."

"Okay." Melody took a sip of soup, then reached for the salt and added a bit of the spice to her bowl. "So, when are we getting a wreath?"

"Wreath?" Sometimes Livia couldn't follow Melody's non sequiters. It was as if her sister went through life only half listening. "We don't need a wreath."

"Mom used to say they're good luck. She always had a wreath." Melody shrugged. "If I had money, I'd get one for the house but you know, I gotta watch my funds."

"I know. You've told me that several times. And what exactly are you saving for?" Livia heard the bite in her tone, but it was too late to take the question back.

Melody scowled. "I don't know yet. Are you getting a wreath? I mean, we have to, don't we? We always did before. You know…Mom always did."

"I—" Livia cut off the sentence when she saw her sister's face. The hope in it, the dependence on her older sister to ensure the continuity that had been disrupted when their mother left. Livia had done all those same things—including buying a wreath every year. "Okay. As soon as we're done with dinner."

A smile curved across Melody's face, one of those peaceful smiles that rarely made an appearance. "Let's go together," she said. "And on the way, you can tell me all about this Edward. And how on earth you are resisting him a second time."

CHAPTER THREE

EDWARD had been standing in the cold for over an hour. One would think a decision like this would be easy to make. His father had pressed fifty dollars into his hand at dinner and told Edward to not come home until he had a little Christmas spirit strapped into the bed of Ray's pickup truck. Edward figured he'd be back home in ten minutes. Fifteen, tops.

"You see one you like?"

Edward turned toward Earl Klein, who had been patiently—or impatiently, depending on your perspective—waiting on him to make a decision. Edward had known Earl for most of his life and couldn't remember a Christmas when Earl didn't work the Methodist Church tree lot. "Not yet."

"Lord, have mercy and send me patience." Earl rolled his eyes. Not one to keep his opinions to himself, that Earl.

Why his father had sent him on this fool's errand, Edward didn't know. In all the years he'd known Ray, his father had never given two seconds of thought to whether they had a Christmas tree or not. Heck, Ray had hardly been home for the holidays, much less participated in them.

Edward's mother had been the one to hang the stockings, toss the tinsel onto the branches and play Bing Crosby. Ever since she'd died five years ago, Ray had skipped Christmas, as if it were just another date on the calendar. No tree, no stockings and sure as heck no Bing.

Then this year, Ray got a bug in his ear and sent Edward out into the cold to buy a tree. Never mind it was only a few days to Christmas and the entire exercise would be a waste, considering a snow pea probably had more Christmas spirit than Edward and Ray put together. They were working men, not sentimental men.

"What are you waiting on? Christmas?" Earl said, with nary a blink at his goofy joke. "Pick a tree already."

Edward waved at the stand of trees. He didn't know a Scotch pine from a Douglas fir. "Pick one for me."

Earl let out a long sigh. "It doesn't work that way, my boy. A Christmas tree is something personal. You gotta pick the one that speaks to you."

"Speaks to me?" He'd known Earl a long time, and though the man had his quirks, he'd never thought he was crazy. And a tree speaking to him—or to anyone for that matter—was crazy. "What's it going to say? Ho, ho, ho?"

"It's gotta say Christmas to you."

"They're Christmas trees, Earl. They all say Christmas."

"Yeah, but which one says it best? Which one is most like you?"

"Uh…that one." Edward waved at the nearest tree. A bluish-green one that tapered up from a fat base. For the hundredth time, he wondered what his father had been thinking. Still, if a tree made his father happy after the last few weeks of hell he'd been through, Edward was willing to put up with the cold and the tree conversations, such as they were. Didn't mean he had to get all merry and ho-ho-ho himself.

"Well, if you ask me—" Earl cut off the sentence, and a grin whisked across his face. "Oh, look, no need to ask me after all. Not when you have a better second opinion right here." He turned, and the gap between Earl and the trees opened up to reveal—

Livia.

Edward had to suck in an icy breath. He'd seen her just this afternoon and should have been prepared to run into her again, especially after Earl had let it drop that Livia was living in town now, but the sight of her tall, lithe body struck him hard in the gut.

She looked great, as if their time apart had agreed with her. She was slightly heavier than he remembered her, but the few extra pounds lent a softness to her features, rounded out her curves, in a way that made her seem more approachable.

Happier.

Damn. That was it. Livia looked happier without him than she had with him. Because of someone new? He told himself he didn't care, but damn it all, he did.

"Don't just stand there gawking at her," Earl said, giving Edward a little nudge. "Talk to the lady."

"Hi, Earl. I'm just here to get a wreath," Livia said to Earl, as if Edward wasn't even there. "Do you have any left?"

"I have a few," Earl said. "But right now, we need a woman's opinion." He stepped back and gestured toward the trees. "Which tree is more Edward?"

"I'm, uh, I'm really not qualified to make that decision. I'm sure whichever tree you choose will be fine." Livia started to turn away, and Edward knew he should let her go. What was it about her that kept drawing him in and making him dream about the impossible?

He'd done that once already today, but the thought of watching her get further and further away from him sent a pain through his heart. What was he doing? He knew what Livia wanted, and it wasn't what a man like him could give. All those words that came with a relationship—permanence, commitment, stability—weren't in his vocabulary.

"Yeah but you know me," he said, working a grin to his face that felt about as real as the fake snow decorating the cashier's register. All he knew was that he couldn't let her leave. Not yet. Not without seeing just a whisper of the Livia he remembered. God, he was torturing himself. "I could use a second opinion. My decor taste runs between hunting lodge and ice fishing shack."

That brought a smile. "I remember."

"So if you have a second, maybe you could help me."

I've missed your smile. Missed your laugh. Missed... everything.

Of course, he'd never say that. He couldn't. She deserved more than he had ever been able to offer.

She looked torn between staying and going. Then she seemed to reach some type of internal compromise and closed some of the distance between them. Damn, she had beautiful eyes. As rich and vibrant as the trees behind her.

"First, it helps to know where the tree is going," she said, giving a little wave as Earl walked off to deal with another customer while they chose Edward's tree.

"In the living room at my father's house."

"Right between his recliner and his gun rack?"

Edward laughed. "You know it."

Livia put a finger to her bottom lip. It was a gesture

he knew well, the one that said she was thinking. His mind darted to thoughts of kissing that lip. Tasting it.

"The Eastern White Pine is too wide," she said, drawing him back to his real reason for being here. "And I think this white spruce is too tall. Maybe try this Douglas fir."

"Sounds like you're talking about the three bears. This one is too big, this one is too tall, this one is *just right.*" He drew out the last two words with a storytelling singsong voice. "I'll take your advice, Goldilocks."

This time, she did laugh. "Well, if you ask me, that one is perfect." Livia started to turn away. "Good luck with the tree."

"Wait." He reached for her, his gloved hand connecting with the thick wool of her knee-length coat. No skin contact, but the sheer act of touching her sent a searing heat through Edward.

What was he doing? He had no call to get involved with her again. He was leaving town as soon as Ray was back on his feet. And from what he had heard, Livia had put down roots in Riverbend. She intended to stay, and he wanted nothing more than to go.

Livia was the kind of woman who wanted it all—the white picket fence, the two kids, hell, even the dog. And he was the last man on earth who should be settling down, never mind doing the one thing Livia had always talked about doing—having kids.

The memory rose up, then hit him, as hard and fast as an uppercut. His little sister, one year younger, and a constant tagalong to everything Edward did. That day, his mother had called out, "Watch out for Katie," as he'd left, but Edward remembered only being annoyed and hurrying deep into the woods to meet his friends. And in the process, maybe lose his sister shadow.

Watch out for Katie.

In the end, he hadn't watched her. Had he?

Edward tried to shrug off the memories but they stayed, stubborn.

"Edward?" Livia's voice drew him back. "Do you need something else?"

He needed her smile. Just one more time. He wanted to be selfish just a little longer and take the balm that Livia's presence offered. Then he'd let her go again. For good. "One cup of coffee," he said. "To thank you for helping me."

"I really need to go. I'm supposed to pick out a wreath and—"

"I can do that, sis." A younger, darker haired version of Livia emerged from the maze of trees. In one arm, she held a plastic carrier with a baby inside—a little girl if the pink snowsuit was any indication. "You must be Edward. I'm Melody. Livia's little sister."

He shook with her. "Nice to meet you."

"We should go get that wreath," Livia said. Her face had paled, and her eyes were wide. She was leaning toward her sister and the baby, one hand out as if to drag them both away.

"I already got one." Melody raised her other arm and showed off a wide circle of evergreen, decorated with a giant red bow and white sprigs of faux berries. "Mission accomplished."

"Okay, then let's—"

"I'll go home and hang this," Melody interrupted, "and you go for coffee with Edward. You deserve a break, sis."

"What about…?" Livia let the question hang in the air. Enough that Edward knew she was discussing something private, something she didn't want Edward to be privy to. He sensed an undertow of something more to the entire conversation. What, he didn't know.

Melody waved a hand in dismissal. "I've got *that* under control. I can handle…it."

"I don't know." Livia looked to her sister, then to the parking lot. "I really shouldn't."

"One cup," Edward repeated, knowing he should let her leave. What was he going to do? Suddenly turn into Mr. Commitment? "I promise to have you home before bedtime."

A flush rose in her cheeks and he cursed silently. He shouldn't have mentioned bed.

Try as he might not to think about Livia and bed in the same sentence, his brain refused to disconnect the two. Because he knew what it was like to hold her long into the night, knew exactly where to touch her to bring that wide, sweet smile to her lips, knew the soft sounds of pleasure she made when he entered her, and knew most of all the warm comfort of her satiated body curved into his. In her arms, he'd found the one thing he'd never found anywhere else. Peace.

Damn. She was temptation embodied.

"Just one cup?" Livia asked.

"We can do some catching up," he said, though he wondered if that was any part of his real reason for asking to see her. "You can tell me about what you've been up to in the last year."

An innocuous conversation, the kind two old friends had. Yeah, that was what he wanted.

Liar.

The baby fussed, her pixie face working up from contentment to a full-out cry. Edward backed up a few steps—not that he thought Melody was going to hand him the kid or anything—but because the whole moment made him uncomfortable. Kids were something Edward had always steered clear of, and for good reason.

The baby's presence reminded him of his last argument with Livia. She'd wanted to know where their relationship was going, and he'd told her nowhere further than where it was. He'd perfected the art of the no-commitment relationship, and that was what he wanted with Livia. No marriage, no permanence, and definitely no kids.

Livia had asked him why, and he'd lied. He'd kept his most grievous sin to himself. He'd been selfish then, too, unwilling to see the trusting, loving light in her eyes dim.

Watch out for Katie.

No, no kids. Not for him. Ever.

Now her sister had a child, and—

The baby seemed to be leaning toward Livia. Before he could think about why, Livia took the child out of the carrier and the pink bundle settled happily into the crook of Livia's arms. And in that second, the truth slammed into him. The year apart. The baby. The last time they'd slept together—

The mirror image—*his* image—reflected back at him, as clear as a summer sky.

Could it be?

His pulse thundered in his head, as he faced the last thing he'd ever wanted. A child.

"I've, uh, been up to a lot. A lot I haven't told you about," Livia said, and her face softened when she gazed down at the baby. Before she even said the words, he knew. Knew what she was going to say, knew what that mirror image meant, and knew the truth. "I'd like you to meet your daughter, Edward."

* * *

The steaming mug of decaf sat between Livia's hands, erasing winter's chill. Beside her, Piper sat in her baby seat, gumming a rattle, oblivious to the tension in the small space. Edward sat across from her, holding a mug of his own. His car, parked in front of the diner, had a green missile-shaped tree now roped to the roof, but Edward didn't look at all as if he wanted to celebrate the holiday.

She could see the stress of the last year in the lines in his face, the shaggy ends of his hair, the wrinkles in his T-shirt. The Edward she had known had always been in control of everything from his appearance to his company. And now he looked…almost lost.

What had she expected, springing that kind of news on him? And what the heck had she been thinking, telling him about Piper when she'd vowed never to do that?

Yet when the moment had come, she'd realized that regardless of how they might have ended things or what he'd said at the end, she couldn't deny him the opportunity to love Piper. She wasn't that kind of woman, and never would be. It was only right that she tell him. After that, it was Edward's choice whether to be involved or not. Right now, she couldn't read him either way.

"I just want you to know, I don't expect you to do anything. Piper and I are doing just fine on our own." There, she'd said it. Gotten the worst part out of the way first.

Coffee churned in her stomach. She pushed the mug to the side. She aligned the silverware. Then the salt and pepper shakers.

"You named her Piper?"

Livia nodded.

He had to swallow hard before he could work any words to his throat. "Nice name."

"You told me a story once, about how you had a relative with that nickname—"

"She was always talking, like a baby bird," Edward said softly. "So we called her Piper."

"It was a sweet story and I always thought it was a cute name. So when Piper was born..." She shrugged and looked away, not wanting him to see that it was partly about her wanting to hold on to a piece of Edward, even when she knew he wasn't coming back.

Edward didn't say anything for a long moment. Then he steeled again and whatever emotion he'd been feeling disappeared. "When did you know?"

Only three other people sat in the diner. An elderly couple in a booth at the back, sharing a platter of French fries. A skinny man in his thirties read the *Riverbend News* while he waited on his order. The room was hushed, as if the entire town was trying to eavesdrop.

"I found out I was pregnant a few weeks after I moved back to New York." She remembered standing in her bathroom, staring at the positive home pregnancy test with a mix of joy and fear. Her first instinct had been to call Edward, but then she'd remembered his vehemence about not wanting children, and put the phone down again. And every day since, she had wrapped this tight cocoon around her and her child. Just the two of them, like a family in miniature. They were just fine without Edward.

But as she sat here, watching the news sink into Edward, she realized she'd been lying to herself all these months. A part of her always had wanted Edward to share in the miracle of Piper. Wanted to see him laugh over her expressions, delight in counting her fingers and toes, marvel at her peaceful, sleepy face.

A part of her had been waiting all this time for some

sunset reunion where they all went off and made a happy family. The sinking feeling in her gut as his features went stone cold told her that wasn't likely to happen.

"Are you sure it's mine?"

Anger washed over Livia in a sharp, fast wave. *It?* How could he call sweet Piper it? Then she took in a breath, and admitted to herself it was a legitimate question. She and Edward hadn't dated very long—just a few weeks—and any man would question an ex showing up a year later, baby in tow. "Yes, I'm sure."

"There wasn't another—"

"There's been nobody but you." The admission slipped out, her temper making her say more than she wanted to.

"Then that makes it mine."

"That 'it' is our child, Edward. She has a name and a personality."

"Forgive me if I'm having a little trouble dealing with this surprise," he said. "It's been almost a year, Livia. You could have said something. You knew how to get a hold of me."

How she wanted to just run out of the diner. But taking the time to gather up baby, diaper bag, car seat and purse didn't make for the fast, stormy exit she wanted. "Like I said, you don't have to 'deal with it' at all. Piper and I are just fine without you. So don't worry about making us another thing on your To Do list. You already made it clear that you weren't interested in the albatross of a child. We'll be fine without you around."

The last had stung. He recoiled, and for a second, she thought he was going to leave. Instead, he signaled to the waitress for a refill, then crossed his hands one over the other and leaned toward her. "Knowing you, I have no doubt that's true. I've never known a more re-sourceful, strong and creative woman."

The compliment took her by surprise. A warm flush flooded her face. Thank God they could be civil about this. In a few minutes, they'd say goodbye and Livia could go back to her quiet life in the little Riverbend house. Maybe send Edward a picture or two over the years. She told herself it didn't hurt at all. That he'd stayed true to his vow not to be a father, not to commit to her, and she shouldn't be upset at all. "Thank you." She moved to gather up her things. "I'll see you around town then."

"I'm not finished." He put up a finger. "But—"

Livia's throat tightened and she stopped moving. But? What kind of *but* could Edward possibly have? She'd told him he could forget about her and Piper. Go back to his life and leave them be. A part of her prayed he'd do just that. And another part prayed harder that he'd do the opposite. "But what?"

"I'm not the kind of man who will abandon my re-sponsibilities."

"Responsibility? Is that how you see our baby?"

"It is a responsibility. Wouldn't you agree?"

"No, Edward, I wouldn't. She's a child. *Our* child. And she deserves to be loved."

"And provided for."

She let out a gust and jerked away from him. "I didn't tell you so you could give me money. I don't want your money. I told you because I thought you deserved to know. In case..." she looked away, bit her lip. "In case you wanted to be a real father."

The seconds ticked by. The tears Livia had tried so hard to hold back began to drop and puddle on the table. He shifted in his seat, seeming to grow more uncomfortable with the silence and her emotions. Beside Livia, Piper mmm-mmmed around her rattle.

Edward cleared his throat. "You know I can't do that."

"You made that perfectly clear before." Acid burned in her gut. Why had she agreed to coffee?

"And nothing has changed in that regard. However…" he steepled his fingers, "I am willing to help you in any other way you need. I am financially stable, and would provide handsomely for both of you."

"I don't want your—"

"Before you say no, think about the advantages." He ticked them off on his fingers, as if this were an accounting program. "The child will be well provided for. Nice home, best schools, everything. If you want to live here, fine. I'll buy you or build you whatever house you want and make sure everything is covered. You and the child will never have a worry."

The reality of his words slapped her hard. "You make it sound like another one of your business deals."

"Think of it as an arrangement. One that takes care of both of you for the rest of your lives."

"And you won't have to get emotionally involved. Be a husband or even a parent to *the child*. No changing diapers, no afternoon feedings, no late night cuddling. But oh, there will be a full bank account. Even if our lives are as empty as air. You can't just throw money at us and hope we'll go away. That isn't how it works, Edward." Now she did get up, thrusting her arms into her coat and grabbing all the paraphernalia around her, scooping up Piper's car seat last. "Piper and I don't want or need your money, Edward."

Then she and Piper walked out the door, the words she hadn't spoken ringing in her mind.

All I ever wanted was you.

CHAPTER FOUR

WELL. That hadn't gone well. Nor had it gone at all how he'd expected.

He'd hoped to handle that with more finesse. To make Livia see the smartest choice was to take his money. The child could have a good life, one where she didn't want for anything.

Anything? his mind whispered.

He ignored the doubts. He wouldn't make a good father, nor a good husband. Livia and the child were better off alone than in a home filled with disappointment.

Still, the sight of Livia walking away, clearly not intending to see him again, hurt. She was angry, and probably rightly so.

Then why had he made that offer? Probably driven by that desperate need he'd always had to make everything right. If Edward had to encapsulate himself in a few words, it would be "the man who wanted to make things right." He had always kept his little corner of the corporate world neat and tidy. Until the fire had shown him how little he had under his control.

Now Livia was springing this…this *baby* on him. He was reminded once again that a split second of acting without thinking could lead to a disaster. One he had tried to contain with money. Apparently, not very well, given the way Livia had stormed out of the diner.

He'd done exactly what she'd accused him of doing—trying to tidy up a loose end with a blank check. Livia didn't understand, though, that anything more, anything smacking of forming a "family" would only leave her angrier in the end. Best to stay detached, uninvolved, by offering only financial support.

He had no business getting involved with Livia again. A woman like that deserved a man who could give her everything—a beautiful home, financial security and, most of all, his heart. Edward could do two out of three. Unfortunately, it was the one he couldn't do that Livia wanted most.

He took a sip of his coffee but the brew had gone cold in the minutes he'd been sitting there. He pushed the coffee to the side and signaled for the check.

"You look like a man who needs a piece of pie."

Edward turned around. "Hey, Earl."

Earl dropped into the seat opposite Edward, without waiting for an invitation. He undid the flaps on his plaid hunter's cap, and laid it and a pair of brown leather gloves to the side. He sent a wave to the waitress, already on her way over with Edward's check in her hand. "Two pieces of whatever pie you have on special today, Annie."

"Caramel pecan okay with you?"

Earl grinned. "Aw, you know that's my favorite. But for God's sake, don't go telling Betsy that. She thinks I favor her blueberry." Annie chuckled and headed toward the kitchen.

"Thanks, Earl, but I don't want any pie. And honestly, I should get going to..." Edward's voice trailed off as he realized his agenda had been clear for a long, long time. "Well, to get some things done."

"You ain't had pie until you've had the caramel pecan here," Earl said. "And believe me, it'll cure most anything that ails you."

"I'm not sick."

Earl arched a brow but didn't say anything.

"Besides, I haven't got time for pie." Edward started to rise.

Earl laid a hand on his arm. "Everyone has time for pie. Sit down and visit with me. Entertain an old man."

Edward sat. He had nowhere else to go, except for bringing the tree home to his father. And right now, Edward wasn't exactly in a deck-the-halls mood.

"So, how's your dad doing?" Earl asked. "I was thinking of swinging by there tomorrow. See if he's up to letting me beat him at cards."

"He's okay," Edward said. "A little down. Some card playing would be good for him."

"Hell, you can't blame the man. A heart attack can bring anyone to his knees. And you know your dad." Earl smiled. "I've never known a busier man than Ray. Hell, he was rebuilding a trannie at the kitchen table the day he got home from the hospital."

Edward smiled. "I remember. He wasn't too happy when I locked up his tools. He told me I was trying to kill him when I told him I'd tie him to the couch if he didn't sit down and rest."

Earl chuckled. "So I take it he's not doing so well with following doctor's orders?"

"What do you think?"

That brought another laugh out of Earl. "I'd think something was wrong with Ray if he *didn't* give the doctor a hard time."

That was his father, through and through—determined to work even if it put his health in danger. Edward had barely seen his father when he'd been a child, and even now, they seemed to…dance around each other, rather than have a meaningful conversation. Edward was nothing if not his father's son—far more comfortable at his desk than in a relationship.

Annie brought the pie and left Edward's check on the table beside his plate. "Enjoy."

"Thanks, Annie." Earl shot her a grin, then dove in to the gooey piece. He swallowed, and his smile widened. "What'd I tell you? Best pie around."

Edward took a bite, then nodded his agreement. He'd eaten here many times over the years, but had never had dessert. For a second, the sweet taste reminded him of Livia, of the peachy softness of her skin. He could still remember how she'd tasted. Of cinnamon and vanilla, or so it had seemed to him, the kind of delicious combination that had him coming back for more and more.

Until he'd realized a union between them was never going to work. That she wanted things out of him that he couldn't give. He still couldn't, even as he'd seen in her eyes that a part of her had hoped for more.

If only she knew what she was asking of him.

He pushed the pie aside, and drained the rest of his coffee, even though it was a cold caffeine sludge that churned in his gut.

"It's great that Livia's back in town," Earl said. "Isn't it?"

Edward tried to act as if he wasn't affected at all by the mention of Livia's name. "Mm," he answered noncommittally. He figured it wasn't going to take much for people to fit together the baby and his past relationship with Livia. But the longer he could put off dealing with that, the better.

Right now, he didn't know how he wanted to handle it. A good man would step up and be a father, create a cozy family of three. Livia had made it clear, though, that she didn't want a semblance of family. She wanted the whole thing or nothing at all.

He couldn't give her that. But maybe they could come to some sort of a compromise that would take care of her and the child. If nothing else, he would make her see the reason of taking his money.

"She's a beautiful woman," Earl said. "Can't believe you let her go."

"It was a mutual decision." He'd broken her heart and she'd told him she never wanted to see him again. As mutual as it could get.

"Well, if you ask me, a woman like that doesn't come around every day. You find one, you should scoop her up, and make it legal soon as you can."

"Then why haven't you proposed to Betsy?" Edward asked. Best way to get the spotlight off yourself…shine it on someone else.

Earl scowled. "I'm an old man. Set in my ways. I don't want someone telling me when to go to bed and what to eat for supper."

"She turned you down, huh?"

"Twice." Earl let out a gust. "That woman is more stubborn than a mule in mud."

Edward chuckled. "Sounds like true love."

A goofy grin took over Earl's face and lit in the older man's eyes. He might complain about Betsy, but it was clear she had stolen his heart. Jealousy filled Edward that Earl had found such an elusive thing as happiness with another person.

"Might be true love. Just might be." Earl forked up another huge bite of pie, but paused before eating. "Anyway, I have to admit, I had an ulterior motive for treating you to some pie."

Edward put a few bills on top of his check, enough to cover the cost of the desserts and a generous tip. "Really?"

"Yup." He ate another bite, clearly not about to interrupt his dessert with talking. Edward waited. And not too patiently. Finally, Earl finished his piece of pie and pushed the plate aside. "I need a favor."

"Anything. You know that." Earl had been a good friend to Edward and his father over the years, acting almost like a second father. The kind of neighbor who shouted warnings when a teenage Edward drove too fast, and offered counsel when Edward had broken up with his first girlfriend. Who'd crowed as loud as a proud father when Edward's company had gone national. He'd always liked Earl and considered him part of the family.

"These joints ain't getting any younger, and with these cold winter days…" Earl shivered. "Anyway, I could use some help at the tree lot. Just for the next couple days. Christmas is just around the corner, and ain't nobody buying a tree after the big man comes down the chimney."

"True." Edward was about to decline, then realized he didn't have anything else to do besides care for his father. Ray was none too happy to be mollycoddled. It was only a matter of time before the two butted heads. Again. Edward's company was in the capable hands of his vice president while Edward was here, and waiting to sell the whole corporation to an interested investor.

What better way to while away those days than by helping a friend? "Sure, I can help out."

"Terrific. You know I love to work that lot myself, but I...well, I need my rest."

Concern filled Edward. Earl had seemed fine, but Edward knew too well how a hearty exterior could mask a bigger problem. "Everything okay?"

"Yep. I'm fine," Earl said. "Just doing too much is all. Betsy and the doc told me to take it easy." Earl glanced away, then gestured toward Edward's pie. "You gonna finish that?"

"All yours." Edward slid it across to Earl.

Earl waved toward Annie and gestured for a drink. "I better get something to wash this down. If Betsy tastes Annie's pies on me when I get home, there'll be hell to pay."

Edward laughed. He knew Betsy nearly as well as he did Earl. She was about as warm and fuzzy as a cactus, but apparently the grizzled auto mechanic had found something to love in the cantankerous B&B owner. Good for him.

When Annie dropped off a glass of water, Earl finished his pie and chugged back the liquid. Then he dropped a few more bills on top of Edward's and got to his feet. "I sure appreciate your help. It'll do you good, to get out in the fresh air. Do something with your day. Besides brooding like a mother hen about things you can't change." He clapped a hand on Edward's shoulder. "You'll be better for it. You'll see."

Then Earl was gone, leaving Edward wondering whether he'd just made a huge mistake or taken a huge step forward.

* * *

"You need to stay in bed all day." Livia crossed to the bathroom and rinsed off the thermometer, then put it on the nightstand beside her sister. "I'll warm up some of the leftover chicken and rice soup before I leave. Do you want a cold cloth for your head?"

Melody flopped back against the pillows. "Why can't you stay home? Who's going to take care of me?"

Livia bit her lip at the whine in Melody's voice. Melody could be so much more self-sufficient, if only she chose to be. Right now, though, Livia didn't have time for a lecture on independence. "I'll only be gone a couple hours. I laid out everything you could possibly need, so all you have to do is stay in bed and get better."

Melody pouted. "Call in sick. Stay here. Take care of me."

"I can't. I'm sorry." Livia left the room and heated up some leftover chicken and rice soup on the stove. As she was bringing it back to Melody's bedroom, she ran through her mental list. Diaper bag packed. Piper's carrier and snowsuit by the door, waiting for Livia to get Piper up from her nap and bundle her up. She laid the soup on the nightstand, beside the television remote, a hot pot of tea and a stack of magazines. "I'll be back before you know it. If you want something special for dinner, text me and I'll pick stuff up at the store."

Melody let out a long, dramatic sigh. "I suppose I'll take care of myself."

Livia wondered if all this was her fault. If she'd babied Melody too much in the years since their mother had left. Trying to step into a role that really shouldn't be filled by a sister. Melody was perfectly capable of taking care of herself, but still a twinge of guilt ran through Livia at the thought of leaving her alone when she was sick.

"Are you sure you know my cell number?" Livia asked. "Maybe I should write it down."

"Livia, you've had the same phone number for three years. Of course I know it."

"Okay." Livia bit her lip, thinking. "There are extra tissues under the bathroom sink and a stack of blankets in the closet—"

"If I get cold. I know, I know." Melody buried herself further in the covers. "I guess I can get up and get them myself."

Livia retrieved a pair of cotton blankets from the closet and draped them over Melody. "Don't forget to shut off the stove if you make more tea. Better yet, use the microwave."

"I know, I know. You are such a worrywart."

Livia arched a brow. "Don't I have good reason to worry?"

"Hey, that flood…thing," she waved her hand vaguely, "wasn't my fault. Entirely."

"Just turn off things when you're done with them, okay? And get well, sis." She gave Melody a quick hug, then headed into the nursery. Melody kept on grumbling, but Livia didn't stop. She'd promised Earl and she couldn't let him down.

As always, the sight of her sleeping baby curled around Livia's heart. She smiled, then reached into the crib. The second her hands met Piper's body, the baby woke up. She let out a little cry at first, which shifted to a gurgle when her blue eyes locked on Livia's. "Hey, beetle." Livia nestled a kiss in Piper's dusting of hair, then held her close.

"We've got work to do today," she said as she laid Piper on the changing table and put on a new diaper. The fresh, sweet scent of baby brushed at Livia's senses, and she paused long enough to give Piper a raspberry kiss on her belly. Piper gurgled and kicked her feet, her hands reaching for—and getting a good chunk of—Livia's hair. Laughing, Livia untangled her hair from Piper's steel grip, and finished dressing her daughter in a festive red and white jumper.

Once Piper was bundled in her snowsuit and strapped into the car seat, Livia headed out the door before Melody could convince her to stay. A few minutes later, she'd driven the short distance across Riverbend, pulling into a space at the back of the church. Such a small thing, to love that everything essential in this small town was located within a radius of minutes. It was a homey, warm and quiet community. She could barely remember the hustle and bustle of New York. And more, couldn't imagine ever returning. This was where she and Piper belonged, she knew it.

Except Riverbend came with Edward, at least for now. He hadn't bought another house, as far as she knew, and hadn't sold his business, either, as far as she knew, so surely he wasn't planning on staying. If he did—

What then?

It wasn't as if they were going to get married. Clearly, Edward was no more interested in a long-term relationship today than he had been last year. How could he have just thrown the money card on the table like that? It was so cold, so impersonal...

So indicative of the man he'd turned out to be. A man who wanted no depth in his life, only fluff.

She didn't want to marry him, anyway, because she knew it would be nothing more than a sham, constructed because they had a child. A mistake, that's what that would be.

Hadn't she already seen how a marriage built on a

shaky foundation could crumble? How unhappy two
people could make each other, even if they had the best
intentions? Leaving their children to flounder in the
wake of bad decisions. The best thing she could do was
stay away from Edward and concentrate on her daughter.

"We're going to have fun today," she whispered to
Piper as she unlatched the car seat. "I'll do all the hard
work, you just sit there and look cute. Which you do
perfectly, if you ask your mama."

Piper blew a bubble and worked a smile onto her
face. The white snowsuit made her look like a bundled
marshmallow, but the jaunty red and white cap on her
head added a burst of Christmas spirit. Livia knew she
was probably biased, but she thought Piper was the cut-
est baby in the universe.

Every day with Piper was precious as gold, a true
gift. She could think of nothing more she wanted.

Nothing? her mind whispered. *Are you sure you're
not missing out on anything?*

Nothing, she told herself. Nothing at all.

Livia propped Piper on her hip, loving the way the
baby's fist curled around Livia's collar. She swung the
diaper bag over the opposite shoulder and headed into
the tree lot. There was a decent selection, considering
how few days were left until the holiday.

Several people milled about the aisles of trees. Then
the group parted, and Livia's steps stuttered. Edward.
Who looked as surprised to see her as she was to see
him. "What are you doing here?"

"Working Earl's shift for him."

"But...that's why I'm here." Her mind circled back to
the conversation with Earl the day before. Had she mis-
understood him? Arrived on the wrong day? No, Earl

had called and asked her to take his shift for the next few days. His exact words, "These joints ain't getting any younger, and with these cold winter days…Anyway, I could use some help at the tree lot." She'd said yes, of course. Earl was a good friend, and if he needed help, she'd be there.

Except if Edward was here. She couldn't work with him. Not now, not when her heart was still stinging from him throwing money at her and their baby, as if that would solve everything. "Well, it seems you have it all under control. I guess I'll come back tomorrow."

"I'm supposed to be working that shift, too." Then Edward shook his head and understanding dawned on his features. He chuckled. "Earl. Riverbend's own Dear Abby."

"What do you mean?"

Edward leaned in close to her so the other people wouldn't overhear. When he did, his breath tickled along her neck and she remembered.

Oh, she remembered it all.

Her pulse skipped, her breath stuttered. She could almost feel Edward's fingers dancing along her collarbone, dipping into the V of her shirt, slipping down her side, over her buttocks, awakening her senses inch by excruciating inch. She'd never known a man who took such time, such care, with something so simple as a caress.

"I think we're being set up." He drew back a little, and she told herself she was glad. "I do believe Earl's matchmaking."

"Oh, he wouldn't." She thought back again to the conversation she'd had on the phone. Earl had asked her about Edward twice and seemed overly interested in whether she'd seen Edward again. The pieces fell into place. She should have known better. If there was one thing Earl Klein believed in, it was that everyone should get their happy ending. "You're right. He is. Oh my goodness. And I fell for it, hook, line and sinker."

Edward nodded, and a slight grin curved on his face. "He's good at it. Very good."

Livia was suddenly aware—very aware—of how close Edward was. Of how her body reacted, even as she willed her hormones to play dead. Of how her heart still leaped at his grin, even as she remembered, too well, how he had broken her heart. She knew even more now how easily he could break her heart again.

Except, in this little snippet of time, she'd glimpsed the Edward she'd met last year, the one who had swept her off her feet. The one with a ready smile, a twinkle to his eye, a tease in his voice. Oh, how she'd missed that. Craved it.

She was immune to those charms, she told herself. Older, wiser. Not making that mistake twice.

She shifted Piper on to the opposite hip and blew her bangs off her forehead. "Well, you can leave if you want and I can handle Earl's shift. Surely there doesn't need to be two of us here."

"And you're going to do what? Put the kid on the ground while you tie a tree to someone's car roof?"

The kid. Not our baby. Not Piper.

Her chin jutted out. "I'll be fine."

He scowled. "Don't be stubborn, Livia. You can't do this alone. I'll stay."

She started to turn away, pressing Piper to her chest, as if their child could be a wall against hurt. But it only reminded her that Edward hadn't wanted the miracle they had made together. Why did she keep hoping? Keep believing in the impossible? "I should go, then."

He reached for her—the second time he'd touched her in as many days—and her heart skipped a beat. "Stay. You're a better salesperson than me. I'll do all the heavy lifting and grunting."

"Like a Neanderthal?" The words slipped out like a reflex.

A slight smile curved across his face. "Ah yes, Neanderthal. I do believe someone once called me that."

She couldn't help herself and laughed at the memory. Did he remember, too? Did he think about their time together? "You *were* being particularly manly that day. Moving all those boxes. And, uh, everything else."

"I remember."

The moment extended between them, heated and heavy. Oh, she remembered, too. She'd been at the banquet hall that day, helping Edward move boxes of files to a storage room. It had been hard, sweaty work, but they had laughed through most of the job, and as the day drew to a close and the last of the boxes were stacked, they had realized how alone they were in the dimly lit, overly warm storage space. Livia had peeled off her sweatshirt, and Edward had let out a slight groan, then taken her in his arms in a crushing, powerful kiss. Boxes had fallen to the floor, papers spilling in a wide circle, but they hadn't noticed. It had been a frenzied rush to have each other, to taste and touch as much as they could, as quickly as they could. Livia had had no idea fast, hot sex could be so amazing and fulfilling.

Now, Edward's gaze drifted down, over her face, then held on her lips. Was he thinking of that moment in the storage room? Was he picturing her arching beneath him, just as she was remembering the hard strength of his back beneath her hands? The blissful, amazing moment when he'd entered her, and brought her to new heights?

An ache built inside of Livia. She had missed him so much. She opened her mouth to say something, anything. Then Piper let out a cry and started to fuss in Livia's arms, and the moment was broken. Livia stepped back. Back to reality, not to things she shouldn't want. But her mind was a foggy mess. "I better get her, uh, something to, uh, play with. You know, a...a..."

"Rattle?"

"Exactly. That darn mommy brain." A nervous laugh, and then she spun away to search the diaper bag on the ground beside her for a toy, any toy, and any reason to avoid Edward's gaze.

"That's not like you," he said.

"What isn't?" She handed the rattle to Piper, who promptly stuck it in her mouth.

"To be so...discombobulated."

"Me?" She let out another little laugh. Why was he standing so close? And why was she still so easily affected by him? She knew better, darn it. "Lately, I never feel like I have anything together."

He smiled. "I find that hard to believe."

His eyes had darkened, his body had tensed, and she could read the message emanating from him as clear as a sunny day. She wasn't the only one remembering that moment in the storage room. She may have thought that history was dead and buried.

But she was wrong.

Piper had leaned over Livia's shoulder, working at that rattle, totally uninterested in the adults. But Livia was interested. Oh, yeah. Very interested.

She watched Edward's mouth. Remembered how his

lips felt on hers. What kind of magic he could work with nothing more than a touch.

And she wanted that again. Very much. She forgot everything else, especially all those very good reasons she'd had for staying away from him. All she wanted now was Edward. "Edward." His name escaped her in a whisper.

He closed the distance between them, until barely a breath of air stood in the space. "You look like you have everything under control right now." His voice was deep, husky and laden with a meaning she knew well.

She could step away. She could change the subject. She could do a hundred things to head off what was coming next.

She did none of them.

His hand came up to cup her jaw and Livia leaned into the touch. Oh, how she had missed him. His thumb drifted over her lips, and she parted them, wanting to taste him, to know him again.

"*Almost* everything under control," he said, his voice a dark growl. Then he leaned in and kissed her.

His mouth didn't just meet hers—it caressed hers. Lips drifting slowly over hers at first, tasting, relearning, exploring. Then his hand came up to cup the back of her head, and he leaned in closer. She yielded to him, opening her mouth, curving into his kiss, his touch.

It was sweet and hard all at the same time, the kind of kiss that made her body sing, her heartbeat dance. She wanted it to last forever, wanted it to end right now.

Before she fell for him again.

Livia pulled back and broke off the kiss. Her body ached in protest. "We…we can't do that," she said. "We're not…"

His gaze still lingered on her lips. "Not what?"

"Together anymore." The two words sounded harsh and cold. Livia stepped back again, and cradled Piper closer to her chest. This was what was important. This was what would last. This was what needed her attention, her full focus. Her child. Not the man who had broken her heart and who would only lead her down a dead end path. At the same time, an older woman came around the cluster of trees and walked up to Edward. Saved by the customer bell. Thank goodness.

"Young man, I could use some help. I really can't decide," the woman said. She was about five feet tall and had a head of white hair that poufed around her features. She clutched her purse to her chest like an arsenal, but had the look of a sweet grandma. "They're all so beautiful. Do you think you could give me a hand? I want a tree that will match my house. It's all done in Colonial style, you know. Which one do you think is best for that?"

"Uh…" Edward shot Livia a help-me glance. He had that deer-in-the-headlights look, and she bit back a laugh. "Livia here would know," he added. "She's practically an interior designer."

"Well, not practically. But I'd be glad to help." Regardless of everything, she couldn't let him flounder through this. And having something to do would keep her thoughts from returning to that kiss, and to what it might be or might not be. She shifted Piper on her hip—it was amazing how quickly such a tiny package could get heavy—then pointed to a short, squat balsam fir on their right. "This one would be great, ma'am, if you have the space. It reminds me of the kind of tree my mom liked. She had a Colonial style home, too."

"Oh, that looks perfect. I'll take it."

A few minutes later, the woman had paid for the

tree. Edward fed it through the netting machine, which wrapped the tree in a bright orange net, then loaded it onto the woman's car. He double-checked the fastenings, then leaned toward her window. "Are you going to need help with that when you get home, ma'am?"

"Oh, what a sweet man. No, I'll be fine. My grandson is coming over to help me set it up."

Livia watched from the sidelines. Edward had had nothing but kindness for the older woman, and patience as she searched her wallet for the correct amount of money, and then her calling him young man.

The Edward she had met a year ago had been charming, yes, but with a Dead End sign around his heart. But had she glimpsed another side of him today? Something more?

She told herself she only cared for Piper's sake. Her sole focus now was her baby, not a relationship. If that was so, then why had she kissed him back?

Didn't matter why. She wouldn't do it again. Period.

After their customer had left, Edward rejoined Livia. "Did your mom really have a Colonial style home?"

"I think," she said. "Sometimes it's hard to remember what it was like before my father got rid of all her stuff." A flood of emotions washed over her and Livia exhaled, willing them away. "It seems it was that way."

"Well, it was a nice touch."

"Thanks. It was the truth, at least the truth as I remember it."

"And did you have a tree like the one that lady bought?"

Livia's gaze went to the distance, to years so far in the past the memories held cobwebs. "I don't really remember," she lied. She remembered the holidays, nearly every single one. The ones before her mother left, when at least there was a semblance of a family get-together, and the empty ones after when her father gave up on celebrating and left his daughters in charge. "When I was a kid, Christmas…well, it was a stressful time."

"It is for lots of people."

"Yeah," Livia said. "But most of them don't leave town after New Year's."

His gaze sought hers. "Are we still talking about your mother? Or us?"

"We have customers," she said, and excused herself to help a young couple select a small, inexpensive tree. Edward let the subject drop and they worked together like that for a couple hours, with Livia shifting Piper from one side to the other as the baby's weight seemed to increase. Melody called twice, complaining that her soup had gone cold, then that there was nothing to watch on TV. Every time, Livia assured her sister she'd be home soon and until then, Melody could manage. Still, she was glad for the interruptions because it kept her from thinking about kissing Edward again. Or about a past that she couldn't change.

When the last customer had left, Edward headed over to Livia. "You should take a break. Sit in the office for a while with…the kid."

As soon as Edward called Piper, their child, "the kid," a reality check hit her square in the gut. He hadn't changed. He hadn't become a family man overnight and he probably never would. One kiss didn't change a thing. Neither did one tender conversation about Livia's fractured childhood. In the end, with Edward Graham, it all came down to practicalities and "responsibilities." To a relationship without messy entanglements.

She didn't want Piper and herself to be a "responsibility." Ever.

"Yeah, you're right. I could use a break." But she didn't mean from holding her daughter—rather from dealing with her daughter's father. And all the disappointments that sat heavy in her chest.

Livia headed inside, stripped off Piper's snowsuit, and plopped the baby in the car seat. Piper settled happily into the rocking base. She sat there, staring at Livia with big wide eyes.

Livia sighed. "What are we doing here, beetle?"

Piper gummed her fist.

"Being around him is torture." Livia plopped her chin into her hands. "What was Earl thinking?"

Piper kept drooling on her fingers, not offering an opinion on anything other than the yumminess of her own hand.

"Okay, well, we agreed to do this for Earl. So we'll tough it out." And, she figured, in the process, she might be able to make some contacts for future events. She made a mental note to bring business cards next time. Once the holiday was over, Jenna would be back from her honeymoon and Livia would join her at the events company, ready to start working on the preparations for the scheduled spring and summer events.

But still, a part of Livia hurt. The part that kept on hoping, like a stubborn sun on a rainy day, that Edward would take one look at his child and fall as madly in love as Livia had. That he would see and understand why it meant so much to Livia for her child to know *both* parents. Even though Livia told herself that her mother's leaving hadn't affected her, she knew deep down inside that it had. There were days when she felt a piece of herself missing, like an aching hole where a tooth used to be. She couldn't redo her own childhood, but she could make sure Piper didn't lack for love.

Her cell phone rang again. Livia knew without looking that it would be Melody. "What's up, Melody?"

"Where's the cold medicine?"

"In the bathroom cabinet. In the box labeled Cold and Flu."

A rustling of objects, a couple coughs from Melody. "Geez, Liv. You have them alphabetized."

"It makes it easier to find things."

"You have too much time on your hands." Melody sneezed, then let out a pity-me moan. "I think my fever's worse. I'm dying here."

"You'll be fine. It's just a cold."

"I think it's worse than that, Livia. I might need to go to the hospital."

Melody had always been like this—every cut surely merited stitches, every sniffle spelled a trip to the doctor, every worry meant something bad was on its way. "I'll be home soon. My shift is almost up here. Do you want something special for dinner?"

"A new body." Melody coughed and sneezed on the other end.

Livia laughed. "I don't think they have those at the Sav-A-Lot. But I'll check."

"Okay." Melody sounded miserable. "Hurry home. *Please.* I'm so tired of taking care of myself. And I'm a terrible nurse. You're much better."

"I'll be home soon," Livia repeated." I promise."

Livia ended the call. At the same time, the door opened and Edward stepped inside, ushering in a cold breeze. Every time she looked at him, though, she felt heat curl in her gut. Darn it all.

Parts of her hadn't forgotten what it was like to be with him. Not one bit.

"Sorry," he said. "Just thought I'd get a cup of coffee while we had a break."

"Okay."

He crossed to the pot, poured a mug, then gestured toward a second one. "Want some?"

"Please." She tipped Piper's chair again, sending a happy smile across Piper's face. While the chair rocked, Livia stretched and worked out the kinks in her back. "For such a little creature, you sure can wear your mama out."

"One sugar and a little cream, right?" Edward asked.

She nodded, trying not to be touched that he remembered such a tiny detail. It didn't mean anything. Not a thing at all.

Edward brought the coffees and took the seat across from Livia. He held the mug between his palms, his gaze on the dark brew inside, and not on her or Piper, still happily gnawing away at her fist. "Can I ask you something?"

"Sure." She sipped her coffee. Edward had made it exactly the way she liked it. Still, in that first perfect sip, she had to wonder if it was because he cared or because he was a stickler for details. It had to be the latter.

"Why'd you come back?"

"To Riverbend?"

He nodded. "I thought you were a New York girl, through and through."

"I thought so, too. But then I fell in love with this town. And when I had Piper," Livia pushed at the chair's base again, and Piper gurgled as she rocked back and forth, "I realized there was no other place on earth where I wanted to raise my child."

"It is a good place for a family." He took a sip of coffee and a long silence extended between them. Tension hunched his shoulders, wrote lines across his face. She waited, sensing he wanted to say something. Maybe something she didn't want to hear.

"I'm sorry about yesterday," Edward said. "I shouldn't have offered you money like that. It was just...I didn't want you to worry about providing for the child. I'm sure being a single mother is hard."

It came down again to practicalities and sensible decisions for Edward. She shouldn't be surprised. He was all about tallying the numbers and weighing the pros and cons.

She glanced over at sweet, happy Piper, and felt a smile steal across her face. When it came to a child, Livia had learned, all those lists went out the window. "The joys far outweigh the work," she said softly. "Piper is a dream baby."

He cleared his throat. "Well, if you ever need anything, you know how to get hold of me."

He might as well have handed her a business card, considering all the emotion in his words. She let out a gust and got to her feet. A happy Santa clock chimed the hour on the wall with a few short notes from "Here Comes Santa Claus."

"How can you sit there, not three feet from your own daughter, and not fall madly in love with her? Talk about her like she's a goldfish in a bowl or a plant in a pot? She's a living, breathing human, Edward, who happens to share half your DNA."

"I know that." He scowled into his coffee. "And I'm prepared to take care of her and you, however you need."

"We don't want your money!" She shook her head. "Are you really that cold? What happened to the man I met last year?"

The man I just kissed. The man I thought still existed deep down inside. Even though I know better.

Santa tick-tocked on the wall, his booted feet swinging back and forth with each minute. Outside, the lights from the Winterfest blinked a bright pattern on the walls. But inside the room, the tension was anything but festive.

"You knew I wasn't interested in marriage or children when you met me, Livia." Edward said. "So don't stand there and act like it's a surprise."

"That was before…" she trailed a finger along Piper's satin cheek and her frustration ebbed, "before Piper was born."

"I can't just change overnight into some goo-goo, ga-ga guy." He pushed away from the table and crossed to the coffeepot, refilling his cup even though it was still half-full. "Don't ask more of me than I can give, Livia."

She heard the pain in his voice, saw it in the set of his shoulders. There was more going on here, something Edward was leaving unsaid. Was it just about the fire? Or more?

The Livia she had been before would have gone to him, offered comfort. But this Livia had one priority—Piper—and if Edward chose not to be involved, she wasn't going to force him. The last thing she wanted was to see her daughter brokenhearted.

Like Livia had been a year ago. Heck, five minutes ago. She steeled her resolve once again. Piper came first. Everything else, even Livia's own heart, was secondary.

"I don't expect anything out of you, Edward. And neither does your daughter." Then she gathered up the car seat and diaper bag and headed back out into the cold.

CHAPTER FIVE

"You look worse than I feel." Ray plopped into his recliner, and picked up the remote. "You watching this?"

Edward jerked his attention to his father. He had barely noticed Ray entering the room, and hardly heard what he said. Heck, he hadn't paid much attention to anything in the last hour. Edward had come home from the tree lot, checked his messages on his cell—and only because he wanted to silence the beeping voice mail indicator—then he'd headed into the living room and… well, done nothing. "Watching what?"

Ray shook his head, then clicked over to a military history channel. The sound of gunfire rat-a-tatted in the background. "What's wrong with you today?"

"Nothing. Just tired."

"From selling a few Christmas trees?"

"No." Though the few hours he'd spent at the church lot had been challenging in other ways, they hadn't been physically tough. He could still see the hurt in Livia's eyes, the hope that he would magically turn into the kind of man she wanted and needed. A part of him wondered if he could, then the realistic side of him remembered that he, of all people, had no business trying to be a traditional family man, much less raise a child.

No matter how much he had enjoyed that kiss—and

damn, he had enjoyed it. A lot. But all he'd done by kissing Livia was open a door to a path he already knew was a dead end.

Edward knew where his comfort zone was—at work. It wasn't in a relationship where he had to open his heart and lay bare his soul. Except in the past year, work had ceased to be the salvation he knew. He felt as if he were floundering, trying to find his footing again.

What he needed to focus on was things he could control. Like unloading the company that he no longer had the heart to run. Then getting the hell out of Riverbend, once and for all. Edward leaned forward on his knees. "I have a buyer for the business."

"Well, good." Then the celebration faded from Ray's features. "That's what you wanted, isn't it?"

"Yeah." Though now that it was a reality and there was a contract sitting in the fax machine, Edward wasn't as thrilled as he had expected to be. For nearly a year, all he'd wanted was the weight of the business off his shoulders. To be free of a responsibility that had become a curse after the fire.

"You gonna take the offer? Or negotiate for more?"

"I think…" he paused, let out a breath, "I'm going to think about it."

He told himself it was because he had so much on his mind. That he was still reeling from the news that he had a child.

A child.

With Livia.

Edward still couldn't quite wrap his head around that concept. He looked at the baby, and looked at Livia, and wondered how on earth that had all come to be. And what he was going to do about it all from this day forward.

Kissing her wasn't the best thing to do. Hadn't

stopped him from doing it, though. Or wanting to do it all over again.

He swore under his breath. He was a mess. No, he'd *made* a mess. The problem was how to clean it up when Livia had made it clear she wanted all—or nothing.

Ray leaned back in his chair and eyed Edward with surprise. "Think about it? You, the son who has never hesitated on anything?"

"I thought I wanted to unload it, get away from the memories and responsibilities, but…"

"That company is as much a part of you as the nose on your face. I know that. Hell, half the town knows that. Except maybe you." Ray muted the television and shifted toward his son. His wise light blue eyes zeroed in on Edward. "What else is bothering you?"

Edward cast his father a curious glance. "Since when did we have touchy-feely conversations?"

"What, a man can't ask how his son is doing?"

"You can, it's just…you never did before."

"Yeah, well, it isn't my best skill." Ray shifted in his seat. "I'm better when there's a desk or something in front of me."

Edward chuckled. "Me, too."

Ray paused for a moment. His gaze dropped to his hands. "Listen, I may not have been around much when you were a kid, but I know you. I see myself in you. The good and the bad."

"Dad—"

"Don't try to sugarcoat it, Edward. I left your mother to raise you and your sister. I wish I hadn't, but you know what they say about wishes—"

"That and fifty cents will get you a cup of coffee." Edward recited his father's favorite saying without missing a beat.

Ray chuckled. "Yeah, and probably not even that in today's economy." He let out a breath, then met his son's gaze. "Anyway, I'm here now, and I'm paying attention. At least more than I did before. And that means I can tell when you got more on your mind than how the stock market did today."

Edward let out a long breath. The information was going to be public knowledge soon, if it wasn't already. He needed to at least tell his father. "Livia had a baby."

Ray arched a brow. "Yours?"

Edward nodded. At the same time, he realized he had no doubts that the baby was his. She looked a little like him, but more, everything he knew about Livia pointed to a responsible and honest woman. "She didn't tell me until a couple days ago."

"Why would she wait like that? I only met her a couple times but she never struck me as the kind that would keep that kind of thing from a man."

"Because..." Edward sighed, "when we were dating, I told her I never wanted to settle down, much less have children. Or anything to do with them."

"Well, that'll do it." Ray leaned his elbows on his knees. "But now the kid is here, so what are you going to do?"

"I don't know." He offered his father a weak grin. "Think about that, too."

Ray snorted. "If you ask me, you're going in the wrong direction. All this thinking is doing nothing for you. You should go see your baby, go to work, keep yourself occupied, instead of running from your responsibilities and sitting around here moping."

"I'm not moping and I'm sure as hell not running from anything. I'm here, taking care of you."

Ray snorted. "And how many days have you spent in the office since the fire?"

"I've been busy, Dad. You know that." Edward's gaze went to the pile of books stacked on the floor by Ray's chair. Not his father's face. Because even Edward could feel the lie underneath his words.

"Yeah, busy running, like I said. Moving out of town, heading to one city after another, then on that foolish trip to Europe, then back here." Ray waved his hands, as if encompassing the whole world in his gestures. "Hell, I don't think you have spent more than a handful of days at work. You used to be there day in and day out."

"My office here is gone, remember? I can't just up and go to Chicago every day, and still be here for you. And why are you complaining? You're the one who just told me you worked too much and lived too little."

Ray waved off that argument. "It's called finding balance, Edward. You can do both. You just gotta keep from having all your eggs in one henhouse. You ever heard of that marvel called the Internet? I hear you can accomplish amazing things with just an email."

Edward scowled. Leave it to his father to zero in on the solution—and the truth. "Pete's doing a good job in my shoes."

"As good as you could do?"

No, but Edward wasn't going to admit that. He'd always been a bit of a control freak about his company, and letting someone else be in charge had never been on his radar. Until everything he worked for went up in smoke, ruining someone else's life in the process. That day, he'd lost his footing, his surety about the way he ran his company, and hadn't wanted to sit behind that big cherry desk ever again. He made a good show at working for a while but really he'd been nothing more than a figurehead. He hadn't rebuilt the banquet hall. Hadn't done a damned thing. Just let it sit. "Doesn't matter. I'm selling."

"As you've said. And yet, you're still holding the reins." Ray got up, and crossed to his son, then laid a gentle hand on Edward's shoulder. "Before you sign anything, think long and hard. Learn from my mistakes. I buried my head in the sand for too many years and missed out on life. On your mother. On you." He gave Edward's shoulder a squeeze. "I regret that, more than I can tell you. Don't do the same thing."

"You were fine, Dad."

"No, I wasn't, and you know it. So quit doing things you're just going to regret later."

Ray headed into the kitchen, his steps slow but surer today than the day before. His father was on the mend.

While Edward was still in an emotional ICU.

Livia considered taking the coward's way out. Feigning an illness or a sudden, mysterious trip, anything other than going back to the tree lot and working with Edward. In the end, it was Piper who decided things.

The baby lay on a pink blanket trimmed with white bunnies in the middle of the living room floor, kicking her feet and waving her hands and just…being herself. Livia took one look at her and knew she couldn't deny Piper anything. Even access to her father.

Piper might be too young to be able to tell one male face from another, but Livia was convinced that Piper had an innate sense that this man was important to her. Yesterday, she had perked up whenever Edward spoke, her head swiveling in his direction, as if seeking the other half of her DNA.

So she bundled the baby up, filled the diaper bag

with bottles and diapers and toys, then headed upstairs to Melody's room. Her sister had spent all day yesterday in bed, and would probably do the same today. A rush of guilt ran through Livia, but she reminded herself Melody was an adult and a few hours on her own wouldn't hurt her. "I'm heading out now. Do you need anything else?"

Melody's eyes were red, her nose even redder, and she had a look of such sheer misery that Livia again considered staying home. "I'm still waiting on that head transplant," Melody said, the words coming out in a thick cold-influenced voice.

Livia laughed. "I'll see what I can do about that."

"Are you leaving the monkey here? It won't be easy holding her while you're selling trees and stuff."

"No. You're sick. You can't watch her, and I don't want her to catch your cold."

Melody pouted. "Truth is, you don't trust me."

"I...I do."

Melody barked out a laugh. "Right. You've never trusted me. The only time you've ever left Piper with me is when she's sleeping."

"Taking care of a baby can be tough. There's a lot to worry about."

"And what? I'm too young to worry? Too immature to handle a diaper change?"

"I never said that."

"You didn't have to."

The silence hung between them for a long time. Livia wanted to take it all back, but she knew her little sister was right. Livia didn't trust capricious Melody with Piper's care. Heck, she barely trusted anyone.

Melody tossed the remote to the other side of the bed.

"There's nothing on TV. I'm so bored." She drew the last word out in one long sound.

"Get something to read."

"Like a book?" Melody's nose crinkled. "I don't think so."

"You know, there are a lot of books out there you might actually enjoy. Not everything reads like an English assignment."

"I'd rather have company." Melody shifted onto one elbow and her eyes brightened with an idea. "I have an idea. Why don't you invite Edward to dinner?"

"For one, I am not dating Edward—"

"Why not? He's sexy as heck." Melody coughed, then dabbed at her nose with a tissue.

"For another," Livia went on, "you're sick and shouldn't be around anyone."

"I'll just lie on the sofa while you guys entertain me." To demonstrate, Melody flopped back against the pillows. "You won't even know I'm here."

"For a third," Livia continued, "if I invite anyone to dinner, it won't be Edward."

"Why not?"

Livia let out a gust and busied herself with folding the clothes that had fallen out of Melody's clean laundry pile and onto the floor. Her sister had never been especially neat, and when she was sick or tired, her room became a hazmat zone. Livia straightened and piled, organizing what she could. "Why don't I get you some books to read?"

"Are you trying to avoid the topic?"

"Of course not."

"Liar." Melody rolled onto her side and propped her head on her hand. "Why don't you want to talk about him?"

"Because there's nothing to talk about."

"There's Piper."

"He's…not interested in Piper." The words choked out of her throat. Finally stating the truth burned. No matter how much she hoped, she couldn't pull off a miracle.

"What? Really? Are you sure?"

Livia nodded. Her vision blurred, and she kept on refolding the same shirt because she couldn't see the stupid seams.

"Maybe there's more to it than you know," Melody said softly.

Livia jerked to her feet and dropped the rumpled shirt onto the laundry pile. "Really, Melody? Was there more involved with Mom, too? Because I seem to remember her just running out the door and never coming back. Like we were goldfish she didn't want anymore."

Tears swam in Melody's eyes and she shook her head. "I don't know."

Livia rushed to the side of the bed. "I'm sorry, Mel. I shouldn't have said that."

Melody refused to look at her. She just shook her head and thumbed through channels on the television. Regret coursed through Livia. All her life, she'd tried to shield Melody from the harsh truth about their mother. As if by not saying it, she could avoid hurting her sister.

"Listen, why don't I go get those books?" Livia said, forcing brightness into her voice.

"Fine." Melody shrugged. "Find me something that won't put me to sleep."

Livia came back with several suspense novels, a half dozen romance novels and a new pot of hot tea. "I'm sure you'll find something you like out of these. I'll be back at five."

Melody waved her off and sank back into the pillows

with a pout. Livia lingered a moment longer, then headed out the door. Livia wished she'd never stepped into the minefield of their mother's disappearance. When she got home, she'd smooth things over with Melody.

The air was crisp and cold, the kind of winter day that hinted at snow. Livia breathed in the clean, fresh air and offered up a silent wish for a little snowfall. She wanted Piper's first Christmas to be perfect—a regular winter wonderland of beauty. Hopefully Mother Nature would cooperate.

What about Edward?

Melody's words came back to her. *Maybe there's more to it than you know.*

What more could there be? He didn't want anything to do with being a father and the sooner she gave up hoping for the opposite, the better.

When she pulled into the church parking lot, she saw that Edward had beaten her there again today. The tree lot was empty, and the festive strings of white lights drooped a bit in the spaces that had held trees just a few days before. Across the street, the town Winterfest stood ready and waiting for tonight's festivities. A miniature village fronted the park, while Santa's Workshop—complete with a real reindeer in a pen beside the shed that housed Mr. and Mrs. Claus, played by CJ and Jessica Hamilton—sat in the back, waiting for the magic time when the sun set and the lights came on, and the Christmas world came alive. CJ, a former set designer, had turned the Winterfest into a destination for Riverbend and all the surrounding communities. She'd heard attendance this year was nearly double last year's. Maybe tonight Livia would take Piper over there. Piper wouldn't know who Santa was, of course, but she'd love the bright lights and Christmas music.

Right now, though, Piper wasn't loving anything. As soon as Livia stopped the car, Piper started crying from her seat in the back. Her face reddened. Her fists pumped, and she let out a wail that seemed to echo in the enclosed space.

"Hey, hey, what's the matter?" Livia got out of her side of the car and came around to unbuckle Piper, who was working herself up into a bigger fit. Livia sighed. It looked to be a grumpy baby day, not nearly as easy as yesterday. She tugged Piper out of the car seat, slung the diaper bag and seat's handle over one arm, then carried Piper in the other. Maybe a few minutes against her mother's side would soothe her.

And if not, maybe they'd get lucky and have few customers. With only a handful of days remaining until Christmas—and even fewer trees left to choose from—chances were good there wouldn't be too many people shopping today.

Piper fidgeted against Livia's hip as she carried her through the maze of trees. Her cries reduced in volume—barely. "It'll be okay, baby," Livia soothed, running a palm down Piper's snowsuit padded back. "Just a couple hours today. Then we'll go home, and I'll give you a nice warm bath before bedtime. Sound like a plan?"

Piper let out a wail. Clearly, waiting for the bath was not acceptable. She squirmed and fussed, her firsts pumping at the air. Livia dug in the diaper bag for a toy—which Piper rejected—then another one, but neither pacified the baby. She rubbed at her eyes and let out another wail.

A middle-aged couple rounded the corner at the edge of the lot, the wife curved into her husband's arms as they walked. They didn't say much, just looked at the trees bordering the sidewalk. Livia increased her pace to reach the center of the lot where Edward surely was, and undoubtedly in need of help. Piper kept on crying.

"Sorry I'm late," Livia said, the words escaping her in a hurried breath. Partly because she was flustered from dealing with Piper, and partly because every time she saw Edward, her pulse tripped. He stood there, tall and handsome, his knee-length black wool coat the perfect offset to his dark hair and deep blue eyes. Beneath the coat, he wore a white button-down shirt and a pair of well-worn jeans, a combination of sexy and business-man that nearly took her breath away.

Why did this man have such an effect on her? Every time she saw him, he reduced her willpower with merely a glance. She'd fallen for those blue eyes once before, blind to his faults. She wouldn't do it a second time. Kiss or no kiss.

"No problem," Edward said. "It's been slow. No customers yet."

It was an ordinary, regular conversation. Yet Livia sensed an undercurrent of words left unsaid, issues yet to be resolved.

Not to mention kisses that had opened a Pandora's Box she'd vowed to shut. Again. Everything inside her—the part that was so used to running from her problems and pretending they didn't exist—wanted to leave. But she didn't. Because the minute she had held Piper in her arms, she had decided to face everything in life from there on out head-on. And that included Edward Graham.

"There's a couple over there by the last few Scotch pines." She pointed and Edward's gaze followed. "Once we've helped them, maybe we could take a few minutes to—"

"You have to take those customers, Livia. I…I can't."

He seemed to have gone cold. He stood as rigid as a statue, his face unreadable.

"What? Why?"

"I just…can't."

Piper twisted and pushed at Livia, and seemed to be working up to another wail. Livia dug in the diaper bag for a pacifier, but Piper wanted none of that, either. She was reaching—

For Edward.

He hadn't noticed, but Livia had. For whatever reason, he didn't want to deal with the customers and she didn't want to trek over there with a fussy baby. A child having a crying fit didn't exactly encourage sales or lift holiday spirits.

Right now, Piper wanted, of all things, Edward. Well, who was she to deny her daughter?

"Okay, I will," Livia said. "On one condition."

"What?"

"You take Piper." As if hearing the offer, Piper leaned even further toward Edward, her arms out, her hands reaching. "She's not in the best of moods and I don't think a crying baby helps make the sale."

His eyes widened and he took an imperceptible step back. "Me? Take…her?"

She nodded. "You can go inside to the office, where it's warm. Just plop her in the car seat and rock her. I think she's tired. Chances are, she'll fall asleep before you can say boo."

Livia knew she could take the baby with her—it wouldn't be an ideal situation, by any means—but as she watched Piper leaning more and more away from her mother and more and more toward Edward's familiar voice, she knew she had to at least try to get Edward involved, for Piper's sake. The little kernel of hope that resided inside Livia held on to the thought that maybe, just maybe, he'd hold Piper and fall as madly in love with their daughter as Livia had.

Maybe.

"I don't know." Edward gave the baby a wary glance. Piper had at least stopped crying, as if she knew she was the subject of debate.

"Either that, or deal with the customers." She shot him a grin. "Your choice. I swear, Piper doesn't bite. Most of the time."

He took another look at the couple across the way. A shadow dropped over his features. "Okay."

She got the sense he was avoiding something, but what, she wasn't sure. She glanced again at the couple out in the lot. They didn't look familiar. Not that she knew everyone in town. Still, Livia couldn't understand why Edward was so upset.

Once again, he had shut her out rather than opening up. Just like last year. Damn, she needed to learn her lesson better.

Either way, someone needed to greet the customers before they got frustrated and left. "You want to take her?"

"Yeah."

A flicker of worry ran through Livia. Melody was right. Livia could count on one hand the number of times she'd let someone else hold her baby. Okay, so she was a bit of a control freak, but Piper was the most precious thing in Livia's life. Taking a chance was simply out of the question.

Then she remembered that this was Edward, the same man who had once touched her so gently, she cried. He would never do anyone harm, and she knew that as well as she knew herself.

And, more than that, he was Piper's father. Of all the people in the world, she was sure he would watch over her safety, regardless of everything else.

"Be careful with her," Livia said.

"Of course." Though he looked dubious, clearly someone who didn't know the first thing about babies.

"If she's still fussy, you can put her in the car seat. Just be sure to latch the strap so she won't fall out."

He glanced at the seat, then at the baby. "Can do. I'll be fine, Livia. Now can you just go deal with those… customers?"

"Sure, sure." What was bothering Edward? He seemed as anxious to leave as a vampire at sunrise. She wanted to ask, but didn't. If anything, his closed and guarded features reminded her that Edward Graham preferred to keep his emotions close to his chest rather than let her into his heart.

She handed over the diaper bag, then the seat, then Piper. As soon as he had the baby, he spun on his heel and headed into the trailer housing the office. He wasn't much of a holidays guy—she knew that—but this was more than just avoiding a little caroling.

He'd shut the door on her as effectively as he shut the door to the trailer. Disappointment curdled in her stomach but she pushed it away. She crossed to the couple, who were staring up the seven-foot length of a reedy pine. "Hi, I'm Livia. Can I help you find something?"

"Well, we're looking for a tree," the woman said, then paused to glance up at her husband. They were in their late forties, and seemed dwarfed by the thick black coats they wore. "I…I think."

"We've always bought a tree," her husband said, his voice quiet. "But this year..."

"We weren't sure." Tears shimmered in the woman's eyes. She looked up at her husband again, and bit her lip. "Miranda is the one who loves trees."

Miranda.

The name clicked in Livia's mind. And then she knew. Why Edward was avoiding this family. Why he'd disappeared inside. She glanced over at the trailer serving as a temporary office for the tree lot, and saw Edward, his back to the window, sitting at the table. Piper's car seat rocked back and forth before him. She couldn't tell if the baby was still crying, but she knew one thing for sure.

Edward was still hurting.

And here was Miranda Willett's family, a visual reminder of the pain the fire had caused. No wonder Edward hadn't had the courage to face them. And no wonder they looked so lost and hurt. Her heart softened, for him, for these people. Another part of her hurt because he had chosen again to leave Livia out of the picture, and let her figure it out herself. What would it take for this man to open up?

"I don't know, Rich," Miranda's mother said. "She told us specifically no tree this year."

Her husband sighed. "I know. But she needs something. I hate seeing her so sad."

The couple glanced at the trees, then at each other. Finally, Mrs. Willett nodded. "A tree it is, then."

"What kind of tree does she like?" Livia asked gently.

A soft, pained look settled on Miranda's mother's face. "She likes the scraggly little trees. The ones nobody else wants."

"When she was little, she was always bringing something or other home," her father said, echoing his wife's expression. "We drew the line at rodents, but let her keep most everything else."

Livia could hear the memories in their voices, the tender love they had for their daughter. She wanted to ask how Miranda was doing, but it was clear that regardless of her physical recovery, she was far from healed emotionally. Undoubtedly, this would be a hard Christmas for the entire Willett family. If picking the perfect tree for them could help ease some of that pain, Livia would stay in the cold for as long as it took. "She sounds like a wonderful girl."

"She is." Then the mother's voice caught and she buried her face in her husband's shoulder. He drew her close and held her for a long time. Finally, Mrs. Willett drew herself up and swiped the tears off her face. "I'm sorry. This has just been so hard on all of us."

"Please, don't apologize. I understand. Let's go find a tree that she would love," Livia said. Miranda's parents nodded, then followed her to the other side of the lot. There weren't many trees left to choose from—a few fat, picture-perfect ones and a couple that had broken branches. Livia circled past those, then stopped by one she had seen yesterday. A skinny tree, shy a few branches of being full, leaned against the church's brick exterior. It looked lonely and sad, like the proverbial Charlie Brown Christmas tree. "We have plenty of regular trees left, as I'm sure you saw, but this one…"

"Needs a little love." Miranda's mother turned to Livia. Tears glistened in her eyes, but they were partnered this time with a smile. Mrs. Willett danced her fingers along the tree's delicate branches. "It's perfect. Thank you."

Livia nodded. Her throat clogged. "I'll get it wrapped up for you."

Miranda's father hefted the tree onto his shoulder and carried it to the register, then fished in his pocket for some money. Livia waved the money off. "No charge."

"We can pay for it."

"Consider it a Christmas gift. Earl would have insisted, I'm sure." She may not have known Earl Klein very long, but she knew he took care of the people of Riverbend as if every one of them was a relative. And if anyone in this town needed taking care of, it was the Willett family.

Livia leaned over, picked up the tree, then tipped it to load it into the netting machine. The big blue metal machine, with its neon orange netting seemed like a relatively straightforward process.

For someone who had used the machine before.

She'd done sales yesterday, and Edward had done all the labor. She hadn't thought to pay attention to how the trees were actually packaged and then loaded onto the customer's cars. In truth, she had no idea how to use it. She wrestled with the machine for a few minutes, pushed this button, that one, pulled a lever that jerked a chunk of netting up into a rat's nest. Finally, she gave up. "Um…let me get someone to help with this…thing."

"I'd help but I spend all day behind a desk." Miranda's father shrugged and looked just as perplexed as Livia felt. "Machinery's not exactly my area of expertise."

"That's okay. I know just who to get." Assuming, that was, that he'd come out here to help.

Edward had to move on past that fire sometime. Maybe starting with something as simple as wrapping a tree could be the first step. She glanced at the Willetts. Would seeing Edward upset them? Or would it give everyone a chance for forgiveness? She thought of the stoic, yet broken man who'd returned to Riverbend, a man she once loved, and knew she had to take that chance. He may never open up to her, but he owed it to himself to move past this tragedy.

Livia took a deep breath and headed for the trailer. A burst of heat greeted her when she opened the door. "Edward, I—"

She stopped talking. Her words disappeared as she took in the vision before her.

Edward stood by the filing cabinets, Piper laying across his arms like a load of wood, while he swayed back and forth. He maintained a distance between his chest and Piper's tiny body, as if he didn't want to quite commit to holding her, but it was a start.

He was holding their daughter. Actually holding her.

Livia's heart flipped over in her chest, and she blinked, sure she was seeing things. But no, it was real. It was Edward.

And their daughter.

He turned when Livia entered. "Shhh. She's almost asleep," he whispered.

"You're…you're holding her. More or less." She stepped closer, forcing herself not to step in there and hold Piper herself because even she knew him just touching the baby was a huge step forward. "But you might want to hold her tighter, though."

"Sorry." He shifted his position but didn't bring the baby any closer. It was as if she were a time bomb and he was hoping like hell she wouldn't go off. "I got kind of desperate when she wouldn't stop crying." He gave Livia a grin, the lopsided smile that he used to have, the one that had made her fall in love with him. And a part of her, she knew, had started falling for him again.

Dared to hope that this one moment could turn into two, then three, then four, then forever. It was only one sliver of time, she reminded herself. It didn't mean anything.

But her heart refused to accept that. Refused to accept the lessons she had already learned. Edward Graham had no intentions of building a relationship of any depth.

Yet she saw how he had looked at Piper in that unguarded moment before he knew Livia was in the room. She had seen the tenderness on his face and dared to dream of more. Of having it all—Edward a part of the circle of her and Piper. Hope was a stubborn thing.

Could this be the part of Edward he had kept hidden from her last year? Fueled by guilt over the fire, or fear of a commitment, or something else? Or was it merely a moment, and nothing more?

"I hate to bother you," she said, "but I really need your help out there. I can't get that netting thing to work."

She stopped short of telling him the Willetts were still out there. If she did, she was afraid he'd say no without even giving the encounter a chance.

"Can do. Uh, but what about…?" He gestured with his chin toward the sleeping Piper.

"Don't disturb her until you absolutely have to. That's always worked well for me." Livia smiled, then noticed the slight grimace on Edward's features from the awkward extra weight. "Except, well, I bet that position is a bit uncomfortable. Here. I can take her from you if you want."

"Sure." He cleared his throat, then transferred the baby to Livia. "She was getting heavy anyway."

And as Edward handed his daughter back to Livia, he transformed again, his features wiped as cleanly as an eraser on a chalkboard. In one second, he went from the soft man with a tender spot in his heart for the sleeping baby in his arms to the distant man who had told her he had no business being a family man.

Then. Or ever.

CHAPTER SIX

EDWARD WATCHED THE baby curl into Livia's chest, like a puppy settling onto a bed. Tenderness filled Livia's face, warmed her eyes. The love between mother and daughter was clear, and for a moment, he felt an emptiness, as if his arms had been severed and he had lost a part of himself. He'd had a few minutes there—a window of time, really—where he'd considered…

Considered things a man like him had no business considering.

What had he been thinking? That he could just step into the father's role, merely because he shared some DNA? He couldn't give Livia or the child false hope like that. It wasn't fair to either of them. He wasn't a man who opened up, settled down. Even if for a minute, he'd thought—

Didn't matter. He'd do well from here on out to act less and think more.

Except, he wasn't really thinking about the hard stuff, was he? He was avoiding it today, as much as he'd avoided it a year ago. Doing what he did best—everything but delve into the recesses of his heart.

He cleared his throat. "What do you need help with?"

Livia cupped the back of her daughter's head with a gentle touch, as if she was shielding Piper from Edward's sudden indifference. He didn't know if she realized the change in her body language or not, but he couldn't blame her. He'd made his position clear.

"I don't know how to work the netting machine," Livia said. "I think I got the tree stuck inside it. Or the net. Something is, anyway."

"It's persnickety. I can fix that." This was the role where Edward felt most comfortable—solving problems, getting things running smoothly again. Dealing with relationships and children, not so much. He told himself it was better this way. Better for him, better for Livia, and most of all, better for the child. Still, a sense of loss hung in the air around him.

Before he took a step, Livia laid a hand on his shoulder. "Wait. You should know that it's the tree Miranda's parents bought. I wasn't going to tell you, but then I realized it would be wrong to have you walk out there and not know."

Just hearing the girl's name again drew him up short. He glanced out the window and saw the Willetts standing by the register, huddled together in the cold. Just like they had been that day.

Edward sucked in a sharp breath, but it didn't stop the mental images. The Willetts, huddled together, unaware of the dusting of snow and ash coating their hair, their shoulders. They stood outside the burning hell of the Riverbend Banquet Hall, staring at the charred skeleton that held their daughter's body hostage. The screaming had stopped, and that was the worst part. The silence that filled the spaces in between the firemen's shouts, the noise from the hoses and the crackle of the flames.

Three firemen dove into the building, while everyone held their breath and prayed for a miracle. After what seemed like an interminable wait, they'd emerged, Miranda a limp doll in the arms of the first man. The Willetts had rushed forward, and the EMTs sprang into action. The Riverbend fire chief had cornered Edward, and by the time he'd finished answering the chief's questions, the Willetts were gone.

All that day and the next, he'd told himself he needed to go see them and Miranda, to apologize. But when he got inside the hospital in Indianapolis and saw the phalanx of friends and family waiting outside Miranda's room, it had been like a wall saying, "Stay out." Miranda had been a popular girl at Riverbend High, and the paper covered her injuries and recovery for days afterwards. Every story was a reminder to Edward of how he had failed. How his bad choices had resulted in years of suffering for the vivacious Miranda.

He'd left town after that. Leaving the words he wanted to say tucked inside him, where they'd done nothing but eat away at his conscience.

"Do you want to talk about it?" Livia asked. "I know this has to be hard."

"No, I don't want to talk about it. What is it with people thinking that if you talk something out, it'll get better? There's nothing I can say that can make what happened go away."

"I didn't mean—"

"What am I going to say to them, Livia? 'I'm sorry for ruining your daughter's life'?" He turned away from the window. "'For making every holiday for the rest of your lives a painful reminder of what happened'?"

Livia's hand trailed down his arm, until she was holding his hand. It was a comforting gesture, nothing more, but still, Edward could feel every ounce of that contact in each pump of his heart. She wanted him to open up, to push past his guilt. She didn't understand that if he let that wall come down, he'd fall apart.

"Tell them you're sorry," Livia said, her green eyes steady on his. "Start there."

"I'm sorry?" He shook his head and broke away from her. "That's not nearly enough."

"No. But it's a start. And you have to start somewhere." Her face held kindness, understanding, encouragement. Concern, care. A hundred things that other people showed and felt, that allowed other people to move forward, live full lives.

Everyone but him. He wasn't built that way, he wanted to say, but Livia's steady support kept on contradicting him. Even last year, she'd wanted him to *talk* about it. To work through his guilt with her by his side. It sounded all so simple, so ordinary. But he lacked the wiring to be that kind of open person.

No, he worked better on his own. Alone. Not in tandem.

Livia had crossed to the door, clearly intending to go out there with him. "You stay here," he said. "Keep the kid warm. I'll handle it."

He walked outside before she could argue. As much as he wanted her there, he knew two things—one, he was better facing this alone, and two, the more he got used to having Livia around, the more he'd start reconsidering a relationship. Not a mistake he could afford to make.

Edward buttoned his coat and headed for the netting machine. Livia's advice came back to him, but when he reached the Willetts and opened his mouth to speak, instead, he said, "Can I help you?"

It took a second for Richard Willett to recognize

Edward. When he did, steel filled his gaze. "What the hell are you doing here?"

"Working the lot. Livia said you needed help getting the tree bundled."

He'd had a hundred things he wanted to say to the Willett family, and none of them included the words *lot, tree* or *bundled*. But he couldn't seem to find a way to get around to the right words. They lodged in his gut instead. Again.

"We don't need your help." Richard started to tug on the tree, but it refused to budge. One of the branches had gotten jammed in the netting machine. Beside him, Alicia, Miranda's mother, watched the exchange.

"Let me get that," Edward said.

Richard let out a low curse and looked away. His wife put a calming hand on his chest, but it did little to temper the red in his cheeks or the hard set of his jaw.

Edward reinserted the tree, attached the clamp hook to the base, then turned on the machine. In one smooth, slow movement, it pulled the tree through the attached funnel, wrapping the bright orange net around the branches at the same time, sealing the entire tree in a neat, portable package. When it was done, Edward cut the end of the net, tied it off, and hoisted the tree onto his shoulder.

The Willetts hadn't said a word. The entire operation took only a few seconds, but to Edward, the heavy silence made it seem like ten hours. "Do you want me to carry this out to your car?"

Richard Willett reached over and took the tree from Edward. "I think you've done enough. Don't you?" Then he turned and headed for his car, with his wife hurrying to keep pace.

When their car peeled away and disappeared down

the street in a flash of red lights, Edward didn't think about the tree lot. About Livia. About anything other than leaving.

Damn. He thought he'd dealt with what happened. Given the sharp slice of guilt shredding his insides, he hadn't. At all.

He crossed the street, walking at a fast clip, trying to put as much distance between himself and his memories as he could. Unfortunately, he didn't think Riverbend— hell, the entire world—was big enough for that.

There were times when Livia wondered if Earl Klein possessed psychic abilities. Within five minutes of Edward stalking off the lot, Earl had pulled into the parking lot. Livia had been standing in the trailer, debating how she was going to run the lot literally single-handedly, with Piper in her arms, when Earl came striding into the tree lot's office, wearing a friendly smile and that silly plaid hunter's cap of his. "How's it going?" he asked.

"Slow today. Just one sale so far."

"It's the end of the season. Most folks have either bought their trees or are waiting till Christmas Eve." Earl looked around the trailer. "Where's your partner in crime?"

"He, uh…had to leave." Livia unstrapped Piper and held the sleeping baby against her.

"Well, that ain't right. I'm sure you and the pipsqueak here," at that, he tapped Piper's nose, "could sell all the trees just with a smile, but you need a man to do the heavy lifting."

"I can—"

"You may be a super woman, Miss Livia, but you

ain't Superwoman." He leaned in and nodded his own agreement. "Looks like I showed up just in time."

"I thought you were taking a few days off."

Earl waved off that suggestion. "You know what happens when a man has too much time on his hands?"

She shook her head.

"He watches too much TV. Every time I turn around, there's another bunch of overindulged teenagers raising a ruckus on a beach. Or a judge telling some fool what he already knows. That he's an idiot."

Livia laughed. "Everyone gets their fifteen minutes."

"Yeah, but no one said I had to watch it." Earl scowled. "Which is why I'd rather be out here with the trees."

"A little help would be nice," Livia admitted. She shifted Piper's weight against her chest. Asleep, the baby seemed to weigh a hundred percent more. She wasn't looking forward to carting Piper all over the tree lot during her nap, but she'd promised Earl she would help.

"You have a more important job to do besides sell a couple trees," Earl said. "You gotta go find Edward and talk some sense into him. I saw the Willetts leaving." He let out a heavy sigh. "Couldn't have been easy on Edward."

"It wasn't." She told Earl about what had happened with the Willetts, about giving them the tree, then getting it stuck in the machine and sending Edward out to help.

Earl nodded. "That was mighty nice of you, with the tree."

"I'll pay for it myself," she said. "I just didn't think it was right to charge them."

Earl dismissed that notion. "You did exactly what I

would have done." Then he sighed. "Poor Edward. That poor boy is suffering."

"Yeah." She thought of how Edward had looked when he'd walked away. Shoulders hunched, head down. She hadn't heard the entire exchange with the Willetts, but had watched it from the office and knew it hadn't gone well. Regardless, she wasn't about to go track Edward down. He'd made it clear a year ago, and again today, that he had no intentions of talking about his emotions. She'd just be pushing against a wall. "I should stay and help you. If you get busy—"

"My Betsy's coming to give me a hand. I called her just before I came in here, figuring you'd say that." Earl grinned. "Seems to me you've plum run out of excuses to stay."

"I—" She saw the determination in Earl's eyes and conceded defeat. She knew it wouldn't do any good, but she suspected Earl wouldn't believe her. "Okay, I'll go."

"Good." Earl picked up Livia's coat and held it out to her. "No better time than now."

"Piper really should finish her nap. I'll go later."

As if on cue, the trailer door opened again and Betsy stepped inside. She shot Piper a smile first, then seemed to realize Livia was there and gave her a smile, too. Clearly, Betsy's heart had already been stolen by the little bundle of pink and white.

"I'm here to help," Betsy said. "And I'd like to start helping with that little precious one right there."

"Oh, I don't know…" Livia knew Betsy well enough and had let her hold Piper a few times when she'd run into Betsy at church or the market. But leaving the baby here? Her protective mother instincts came roaring forward, even though she knew Betsy and Earl and knew they considered Piper an adopted grandchild. Seemed lately the entire world was out to prove Melody right and to put Livia to the test. "She can be a handful."

Betsy parked a fist on her ample hip. "She's no such thing. Why, that Piper is the most beautiful and perfect baby in the world."

Livia laughed. "Okay." Deep inside, she knew Earl and Betsy would care for Piper, guard her like two tigers with a newborn cub. She handed over Piper, feeling the familiar tug of sadness every time she let Piper out of her arms. "The diaper bag is over there, and if you want, she can sleep in her car seat."

"We'll be fine. Don't you worry." Betsy had already settled into the office chair and was leaning back, with Piper snuggled close. The baby, adept at sleeping most anywhere, curled up on Betsy without waking.

Livia brushed a gentle kiss across Piper's head. "Thank you."

"No, thank *you*," Betsy whispered. "Holding this little girl is like holding a slice of heaven."

Livia smiled, and turned to Earl. "You sure you don't need me to stay?"

He shook his head. "Edward needs you more. That man's hurting, and he needs a friend."

She sighed. "I know. But I don't think I'm the friend he needs." But she buttoned her coat and stepped out into the cold anyway. Because she knew no matter what had happened between herself and Edward, if he needed her, she would be there.

Even if doing so broke her heart.

It was a long time before Edward even noticed the cold. He'd walked far and fast, and when he reached the edge of Riverbend, he'd turned around and walked back. Eventually, he'd have to return to the lot and pick up his car. Winter nipped at the exposed areas around his coat, but he didn't feel the chill. His frustration and anger fueled a fire that couldn't be tamped by Mother Nature.

He didn't realize he'd detoured until his feet stopped moving and he saw where he had ended up. His breath lodged in his throat, and his chest constricted.

Was it ever going to get easier?

He wanted to walk—no, run—away, but his feet refused to move, as if a part of him demanded he look, demanded he see. Demanded he deal with it once and for all.

The fire.

There were still ruts in the ground from the heavy wheels of the fire trucks, forming a frozen moat around what had once been a twelve-thousand-square-foot building. A few timbers stood defiant, like charred stick figures refusing to be downed. Against the stark gray landscape, the remains of the Riverbend Banquet Hall seemed sad and lonely. Forgotten.

But Edward hadn't forgotten. Not when he'd left town, not when he'd gone to Europe, not when he'd put the business up for sale. He hadn't forgotten. At all.

"I can't believe any of it's still here."

He turned at the sound of Livia's voice. "What are you doing here? Where's the baby?"

"Earl and Betsy showed up after you left. They kidnapped Piper and shoved me out the door." She laughed, then sobered and met his gaze. "They insisted on babysitting so I could talk to you."

He scowled. "I don't need to talk. I need to be alone." The wind kicked up and nipped along the exposed parts of him, skating down his back. Surely the biting cold bothered Livia, too, but she didn't show it. Nor did she leave.

"Do you think maybe that's part of the problem?" She took a step closer. There was no escaping those wide green eyes and a gaze that he swore could see right through him. "All that being alone, and no talking?"

"What problem? I don't have a problem."

She pursed her lips and didn't say anything. It was the same argument they'd had last year. Always, Livia had pressed him to talk, to open up, and he had resisted. He preferred to retreat, to deal with things himself.

Except, what good had it done him over the past year to deny and ignore? It hadn't made anything better. In fact, he was pretty sure he felt worse now. Especially after letting a year pass without doing a damned thing or speaking up. He'd walled himself off and ended up alone. Miserable.

"Okay." He let out a sigh. "Maybe you have a point."

They didn't say anything for a long while. The guilt kept churning in his gut, didn't go anywhere. Livia stood beside him, staring at the same bleak scene. Her mere presence offered a comfort and peace. "What happened that night?"

A bird flew overhead, letting out an angry squawk at the intruders. A car drove past them, wheels crunching on the cold, ice-dusted road. Above them, clouds formed in puffy poodle-like bunches, floating in a pack across the sky. But before him, the world had stood still, caught in a tragic, year-old time warp.

Was he stuck there, too? Was that why he kept trying to shed everything that once used to matter so much to him? First, his relationship with Livia, then his home in Riverbend, then his business? If he talked about it, if he began to exorcise those demons, maybe he could move out of this cement-filled purgatory.

But still he couldn't speak.

"A year ago, you didn't want to talk about it," Livia said.

"I deal better on my own."

"Do you?"

Winter held the question tight in its frosty grip. Did he? Had he? Really?

He'd pushed her away once, and here he was, back in nearly the same place all over again. Circling, circling… and never moving forward.

"I had gone home around six that night," he said finally, the words seeming to come of their own volition, as if his voice was overriding every other part of him. "We had a wedding scheduled for the next afternoon, and I wanted a little time off before coming in to run that. I didn't always run stuff, you know?"

She nodded.

"But the bigger my company got, I found I liked taking over from time to time. It was like getting back to my roots. So when I was in Baltimore, I'd spend a night or two running the concert hall. Or work concessions at the stadium in Boston. It kept me grounded, kept me in touch with the company."

"I remember you telling me that."

"Riverbend was where I liked to be best, though. This was my first property. Every time I got out from behind my desk, it was like those early days all over again." Or it had been, at least, before…

"Miranda and a few other employees stayed late to handle a small party," Edward went on, the words scraping past his throat, but not stopping. "A celebration for a local band that had made its first CD. Nothing big, and I figured they could take care of it. And since I was overseeing the wedding on Saturday, I wanted to cut the night short." He closed his eyes, and it was like he was there again. Heading out the door, a hurried goodbye over his shoulder. The door closing, the banquet hall forgotten—

Until the call from the fire department at one that morning.

He didn't want to continue. He wanted to keep all of this…this pain and regret locked inside him, but what good had that done him? Facing it was harder, but in the end, would it be better?

Maybe.

He thought of his father, who had waited until his late fifties—and a massive heart attack—to start opening up. Did Edward really want to repeat that?

"I went home, went to bed early," he went on. All this time, he hadn't talked about it to anyone other than the firemen who'd interviewed him that night. And now it seemed like the words were practically tripping over his tongue in their rush to be out in the open. "It had been a hard week—I'd had to let go a manager at one of the Chicago facilities, and had spent half the day renegotiating the lease on the Indianapolis property. I was stressed, and tired, and just didn't want to deal with anything." His breath frosted in a cloud around his face, but he barely noticed the dipping temperatures or the graying sky. "I should have stayed."

"But you said it was a small party. Surely something the employees could handle, and normally did."

"Normally, yes, they could have. But it was an inexperienced staff, and I should have known better. The facilities manager was new, too, and I should have stayed, did a double check." He took a few steps forward, crossing over the border of frozen mud ridges and up to what had once been the front door. "Damn it. I should have known."

Livia was beside him, her hand on his shoulder, her presence almost a balm. "You can't predict the future. Not then. Not now."

He shook his head, unwilling and unable to release himself so easily. The regrets held tight to him, a band around his chest, a thick fist in his throat. But still he kept talking. "The band stayed late, long after the rental time, and the staff joined in on the party. They weren't supposed to, and they knew that, but a lot of them were friends with the band and I guess they figured…"

"If the cat's away, the mice will play."

He nodded. "Miranda was in the back, putting away the linens and stacking cardboard boxes to go out with the trash, when—" he shook his head, trying to erase the images, but they stayed, stubborn "—a frayed electrical cord caught fire. Apparently the band brought their own equipment and one of the cords wasn't in the best of shape. Normally, I would have checked that kind of thing if I was there. But I had gone home and the manager was inexperienced…" He let out a curse. "The fire spread quickly, igniting the cardboard, and…in seconds, the whole building was on fire. Everyone got out right away, everyone except…"

He couldn't say it, couldn't finish the sentence. He closed his eyes and he saw the slim nineteen-year-old, her eyes wide and frightened, seeing no escape from the encroaching fire. He had dreamed that image a thousand times in the year since the fire. Heard her terrorized scream in his ears, as if he'd been there.

"Richard ran for the building," Edward said, softer now. "He was screaming his daughter's name, determined to find her himself. The firemen pulled him back, but he kept lunging for the building. Then three firemen went in and God, it seemed like forever before they came back out. Smoke was coming off her body, Livia. Smoke." Edward shook his head, pinched at his eyes. "Damn it. Damn it all to hell."

Livia's arm went around his shoulder, her head against his chest. "It wasn't your fault."

He tried to pull away but Livia held firm. "I was the owner. Didn't matter how big the company was, or how much time I spent behind a desk. In the end, I was the one responsible. I should have made sure everything was okay. And now that girl can't go to college or do anything. Do you know she wanted to be a graphic designer?"

Livia shook her head.

"Something in the music industry. Album covers or something. I remember her telling me when she came in for the interview. How that would let her combine the two things she loved most—music and art. And now…" He closed his eyes and shook his head. *"I should have stayed."*

He'd said that to himself over and over since that night. If only he had stayed. If only he had double-checked the band equipment himself. If only he had kept the promises he'd made.

But he hadn't. And this time, Miranda Willett had paid the price. He couldn't even think about the pain and suffering she had endured every day since that night. If he did, he had a feeling he'd fall apart, and not be able to put himself together again. If he could trade places with her—for a day, for a month, for eternity—he would.

"You can't be anywhere twenty-four hours a day, Edward. No one can be."

He shrugged off her touch and crossed to the streaked cement foundation. In a few steps, he stood in the center of the hall, or what had once been the center. A year ago, the Riverbend Banquet Hall had been booked nearly every day. It had been one of several shining stars in his business constellation. He'd thought he had the world by the tail, when really he hadn't had anything at all.

He bent down and curled his fist around a charred piece of wood. It crumbled in his grasp, turning to ash with one touch. He cursed again. The regrets crowded around him, squeezing at his chest. "She suffered that day and every day since," he said, his words a harsh rasp, "and that's all my fault."

"It was an accident. Surely you know that." Livia came around to face him, forcing his gaze to focus on her face, instead of the burned shell of the building. Her deep green eyes bored into his. "Oh, Edward, Why don't you believe that?"

"I…" His gaze darted back to the devastation before him. A minute more, and Miranda would have died. That bright, vibrant girl, permanently hurt because he had gone home early. That was what he hadn't been able to say last year, and even now, he still couldn't. "I can't."

"If you don't, you can't move forward. And you need to move forward, Edward. Not just for you, but for our daughter, too." She reached for him, and he saw the hope in her eyes, the belief in him.

She didn't know everything, though. Didn't know how he had let people down, over and over again. This wasn't one mistake. It was many.

Watch out for Katie.

Watch out for Miranda.

In the end, he hadn't watched out for anyone. Except himself.

He jerked to his feet. Better to do this now than to let Livia keep building that hope that someday, he'd turn into the husband, the father she wanted. He knew better than to try to be a part of a family. To be responsible for anyone's child, even his own. He was no good at this, no good at all.

"I'll support the baby financially," he said. "But don't expect more out of me than that."

She reached for him again. "What happened to the man who held Piper and danced with her to get her to sleep?"

"I was just trying to get her to sleep."

"Liar."

She was there, confronting him, over and over. She refused to see that he could be anything other than what he was. He exhaled, and wished he had never come back to town. This was a hell of a lot harder than he'd expected it to be.

Because he knew how painful it had been to excise Livia from his life once before. He wasn't sure he could do it again, especially now that Piper had been added to the mix.

God, it hurt. He steeled himself and tucked the feelings away in the back of his mind. Best to do it now, fast, before he reconsidered. She deserved a man who could be open with her, who could let her into his heart. He had tried—and stopped short of giving her all.

"Stop asking more from me than I can give, Livia," he said, and didn't meet her gaze. Because if he did, he might not be able to finish the sentence. She didn't need a broken man, one who had let down everyone around him. She deserved more. "Money, fine. House, fine. Education, fine."

"This is about more than the fire, Edward." She came

around to face him, those beautiful, inquisitive green eyes. "What aren't you telling me?"

"Nothing." He tried to move away, but she stuck with him. "Why is it so important to you to create some fairy tale out of our lives? To keep pushing me to be something I'm not?"

She recoiled, and he wanted to take the words back. "You think raising our child together is a fairy tale?"

"I think you're looking for something that you didn't have."

Her jaw dropped. Her eyes widened.

And he hated himself.

"You don't mean that," she said, the words a pained, choked whisper.

He was on a train he couldn't stop, the words barreling down a suicidal track. All he wanted was to be away from this place, away from this subject, and most of all, away from everything he wanted and couldn't have. He wanted to retreat to his desk, to the quiet solitude of work. Not deal with the tsunami of emotions whirling inside him. So he lashed out, knowing it was wrong, knowing she and Piper might end up despising him. But if he didn't, Livia would go on hoping.

"Your mother ran off and your father pretty much checked out," Edward said. "You had to raise your sister, and you vowed early on that you would never do that to your own children—"

"I know I said that but I didn't mean—"

"So that's what you're trying to do now, isn't it? Trying to create that perfect family for your child by forcing me into some mold of the perfect father. All so that she doesn't have to know what it's like to go along with just one parent and a well-meaning sister?"

Tears swam in her eyes, and Edward wanted to undo

the damage, but the words were there, and there was nothing he could do to take them back. If he wavered at all, Livia would keep on hoping and dreaming for the both of them. Maybe if she hated him, she'd give up this idea that he could be some Utopian husband and father.

"This isn't the same thing, Edward. Not at all."

"Maybe not. But either way, I—" he drew in a breath and surveyed the decaying remains of his dreams "—I can't be the man you want me to be. I'm sorry."

CHAPTER SEVEN

LIVIA CRIED UNTIL her tears were as dried as her heart. She'd walked away, leaving Edward standing amid the ruins of the banquet hall, and then retrieved Piper, hurrying out of the tree lot before Earl and Betsy could ask her any questions. They'd seen the upset on her face, but let her go without too much prodding. Thank God.

Piper had gone to bed early, and Livia had told Melody she had a headache and was going to bed early, too. Livia's bedroom door had barely finished latching behind her when the tears started.

Why had she thought Edward had changed? Just because of something she'd glimpsed inside a trailer?

He hadn't changed at all. He was still the closed-off man she met last year. The one she had fallen for so hard that she didn't realize until it was too late that he hadn't fallen for her, too.

Deep in her heart she'd always thought he'd change his mind, that what he'd said last year was some kind of knee-jerk reaction to their discussion about marriage and to the shock of the fire. But she'd been wrong. So very, very wrong.

Livia poured more tears into her pillow, but it didn't ease the ache in her heart. She clutched it to her chest, and tugged the blanket up until it covered most of her face. But even here, buried in the dark, silent comfort of her bed, she couldn't find peace.

A soft knock sounded on her door. "Livia?"

Livia feigned sleep. No way was she going to get up to make Melody more tea or help her find the remote or entertain her because there was nothing good on TV.

"I know you're awake. Can I come in?"

Livia sighed. "Can't it wait until morning? I'm… tired."

Melody either didn't care or didn't hear what Livia had to say. She came in the room, and dropped onto the edge of Livia's bed. "Liv—"

"Please, Melody, just let me be. I'll get whatever you need tomorrow." She buried her head deeper into the pillow and prayed her sister would take the hint.

"Liv." Melody paused. "Livia, look at me."

When it became clear that Melody wasn't about to leave, Livia rolled over and looked up at her little sister. In the dark, Melody's eyes seemed wider and lighter. "What?"

"What's the matter?" Melody asked.

She must have heard her crying. "Nothing."

Melody smiled. "Liar. I know that look anywhere. Someone broke your heart. Someone named Edward, I bet."

Livia draped her arm over her eyes. Damn, they hurt. "I just want to go to sleep."

"That's the worst thing you can do. You should talk about it. Sleeping just delays the problem."

Despite everything, a slight smile worked its way to Livia's face. "Where have I heard that before?"

"You said it to me. A hundred times at least. Remember the seventh grade dance? When Ryan

Spartan stood me up? And all I wanted to do was stay in bed and cry and sleep?"

"I made you get up and get dressed."

"And go to the dance and show that Ryan what he missed out." Melody grinned. "Did I ever tell you he spent the entire night in the corner, while his date flirted with another guy? He kept glancing over at me, and I knew he was regretting what he'd done."

"Really?"

Melody nodded. "Going by myself showed me that I could be okay, no matter what. And not to mention, taught Ryan a lesson or two. Which is why I'm telling you to do the same thing."

"Get dressed and go to the dance?"

Melody shook her head. "Get dressed and go to the Winterfest. You've been dying to go, and it's only open for two more nights."

"I don't want to go to that. I'm not in a Christmas mood."

"Because," Melody reached forward, took Livia's hands and hauled her into a sitting position, "you're lying in this bed, wallowing in self-pity."

"I'm not."

Melody glanced at her askance. "I've done it enough to recognize it in you. Now get up, get dressed and show that Edward Graham that he's the biggest idiot to walk the earth."

"I can't go out. Piper—"

"Will be fine with me here. I'm feeling better." Melody smoothed a hand across the comforter. "Besides, I've been thinking. Being sick gives you a lot of time to do that, you know."

Livia nodded.

"And I realized I let you do a lot for me. And you let

it happen." Melody wagged a finger at her. "I…well, it's just easier that way."

Livia sighed. Her sister was right. Melody needed something, and Livia provided it, slipping into the old role of surrogate mother as easily as slipping on a pair of socks. "I guess we got into a routine—"

"And never got out of it." Melody kept on tracing the floral pattern on the comforter. "Do you know why I came here? Instead of going to Dad's?"

Livia shook her head.

"Because I count on you, Livia. Because you're the one who's always going to…" Melody's gaze returned to her sister's. "Well, always tell me the truth. Whether I like it or not."

"I don't do it to hurt you, Melody." She reached for her little sister's hand. "I worry about you, that's all."

Melody gave Livia's fingers a squeeze. "I know. And that's why you have to stop. Worrying about me, that is."

Livia shook her head. "Mel, I can't—"

"You have to. It's time you lived your own life. And stopped being my mom."

"I don't mind."

"I know that. But I do." Melody cocked her head and gave Livia her familiar mischievous smile. "And if you don't let me stand on my own two feet, I'll never learn how to do it."

Livia grinned. "How did you get so wise?"

"Listening to you, sis." Melody reached forward and drew Livia into a hug. "Just listening to you."

The Winterfest was in full swing by the time Livia arrived. She hadn't wanted to go, but Melody had insisted, even going so far as to toss a pair of jeans and a sweater onto the bed and refusing to leave the room until Livia got dressed. Livia had finally acquiesced. Melody was right. Staying in bed and wallowing in self-pity wasn't going to help anything. Piper was already tucked in for the night so Livia left her home with Melody.

Livia wandered the town park, marveling at Santa's village—complete with a real reindeer—and the gingerbread family set up outside a small gingerbread village. She got a pretzel from the vendor stand and a cup of hot chocolate made by the local Girl Scout troop. In the center of the park, she could see a group decorating the gazebo in preparation for tomorrow night's big dance.

Suddenly, it was too much. She didn't want to go to the Winterfest alone. Ever since she'd arrived in Riverbend, she'd dreamed of coming here with Piper. Seeing the delight on her daughter's face as she took in the sights and sounds and got her first picture with Santa.

And yes, a part of her, buried deep inside, had pictured Edward in that little tableau, too. A crazy, impossible wish. One sentimental wish she had hung on to for a long time, because a part of her heart had never let go. He'd never loved her the way she loved him, and yet...

She turned away and headed out of the park. She hit the sidewalk and waited for a car to pass so that she could cross. She was going home. Despite Melody's advice, Livia didn't think going out by herself was working out.

She sensed him before she saw him. The spicy notes of his cologne danced on the breeze, teased at her senses. Edward was here. Behind her. But she stood her ground and didn't pivot toward him.

"I think this is yours."

She glanced over her shoulder. Edward was holding out one of Piper's toys. The small stuffed animal looked so incongruous in his big hand. Behind them, the sights and sounds of the Winterfest continued, bright and merry. "Where did you get that?"

He thumbed toward the tree lot across the street. "She must have dropped it when she was in the office. I found it there when I went back to get my car. I came by the house to drop it off, and your sister said you were here."

And he had tracked her down to bring it to her? Why? It was something that could have waited. Was he just trying to make her miserable? Trying to confuse the issue? Every time she thought it was over, he showed up again. What did Edward Graham want?

"Oh. Okay, thanks." She took the small stuffed giraffe and tucked it into her coat pocket. "Have a nice night." She stepped off the curb and crossed toward the small well lit diner on the corner of Main. Inside, she could see Earl and Betsy sitting at one of the window booths.

Edward walked right beside her. "Not going to the Winterfest?"

"I'm not in a holiday mood right now."

"Me neither. I've never been much for Christmas."

She whirled around to face him. "Then what are you doing?"

"Just out, trying to enjoy the evening. Feels like snow, don't you think?"

"No, I meant, what are you doing with me? What do you want?" She shook her head and stopped walking. She could feel the tears rising up again. She blinked, willing them away. "Just stop, Edward. I'm not a yo-yo that you can jerk back and forth." She turned away again. And waited for him to leave.

He didn't. "I'm not trying to jerk you back and forth. I…" He let out a long breath. "I can't let it end like this."

"End? When did we begin?"

"A year ago. Or have you forgotten? And now we have a child."

Still, "a child," not our child or our baby. "I'm not having this conversation." She started to move away, but Edward grabbed her arm.

"I was out of line earlier today, Livia. I'm sorry." He dropped her arm, and moved back, as if he finally realized she didn't want him to touch her. "I shouldn't have said half of what I said."

"Then why did you say it?" Now the tears choked in her throat.

He looked past her, at something far in the distance, something, she suspected, didn't even exist in this time, in this place. "It's a long story."

She wanted to tell him too bad, it was too late, but that stubborn cloud of hope in her chest refused to give up on Edward Graham so easily. She had glimpsed something in him, something real and true, as if he had pulled back a curtain. All this time, she'd thought Edward was a cold man, incapable of love, then she'd seen him this week, being kind to an elderly woman, dancing with Piper in the trailer and opening his heart at the ruins of the banquet hall. Was there more? "So tell me."

"Not here. I…" He let out a breath. "I just want to forget all that tonight." He put out his hand and nodded toward the diner. "Grab some coffee? Some pie?"

What was she thinking? Go with him? After she had just spent the better part of the evening crying over him? She was out here to forget him, not take the same wrong turn again. No matter what unguarded moments she might have seen, in the end, it came back to the same answer.

Edward wasn't a settle-down kind of guy and she wasn't dumb enough to let him break her heart a second time. No. There'd be no pie. And no more silly hope.

"I don't think that's a good idea." She tugged her hand out of his. Then Livia hurried away, before her common sense was overridden by heartbreak.

Edward should have gone home. He fully intended to do that, after that insane attempt to make up to Livia. Did he really think a piece of caramel pecan would be enough to heal the wounds he'd made?

He had thought he'd done the right thing when they'd been standing outside the remains of the banquet hall. He'd broken it off, severing that tie once and for all, and telling himself it was the best thing for all of them. He'd done it once before, he could do it again. Even if it hurt ten times more the second time.

Then he'd found Piper's toy on the floor of the tree lot office, and his mind had rocketed back to holding his daughter, to the soft comfort of her strawberry-scented skin, and he'd realized something.

No matter how hard he tried to push Livia away, how hard he tried to avoid being a father, that little pipsqueak had already grown in his heart. He missed her, damn it, and missed her mother most of all.

But he'd messed everything up. Every time he tried to make it better, easier, really, it got worse. For a man who had successfully built a mega business from the ground up, he was having a lot of trouble with something so simple as relating to one woman. What was it about him that made it almost impossible to open his heart?

She'd asked him what he wanted. It was a question he still couldn't answer. All he did know was that he didn't want to let go of Livia, not yet. For her sake, he should stop. Walk away—and keep walking. Simply by holding on, he hurt her.

But as he headed toward his car, his steps made a detour and he found himself in the parking lot of the Methodist church. A handful of trees remained, lit by the string of lights that surrounded the tree lot. The sales office had shut down an hour or so earlier. A small hand-lettered sign—complete with a greasy thumbprint that undoubtedly belonged to Earl—was propped up in the trailer's window. TOMORROW IS CHRISTMAS EVE! GET YOUR TREE IN TIME FOR SANTA'S VISIT! OPEN AT NINE A.M.

The lot was quiet, peaceful, with just the soft under-tow of the music from the Winterfest playing in the air. It was as if the world had stopped on Christmas Day in this little corner of Riverbend.

Edward rounded the corner and found Livia stand-ing beside a lone, skinny pine tree. She reached out and slid a hand down one of the branches. A few needles dropped into her palm, then drifted to the ground.

He hesitated. The golden light of the streetlamp framed her and cast a soft glow over her delicate fea-tures. She had an ethereal quality to her, as if at any mo-ment she could disappear. He wanted to reach out and hold her. But he didn't. "Livia?"

She turned and jerked a bit in surprise. "Edward. What are you doing here?"

He shrugged and moved closer. "I didn't want to go home. My dad is probably asleep in front of the TV, while some war movie blasts his eardrums. And I wasn't in the mood to be my only company."

A bittersweet smile stole across her face. "Me either."

He took another step closer to her. In the darkened, intimate confines of the tree lot, he was a hundred times more aware of her. Of how close she was, how alone they were. How far apart they'd drifted in the last year. Even as he knew he shouldn't, he wanted to close that gap, to have a taste of that happiness just one more time. "Are you thinking of buying a tree?"

She shook her head. "I already have one. And a wreath, thanks to my sister. Got the house all Christmas-ed up."

There was a melancholy note in her voice. He took another step, and now he could catch the fragrant notes of her perfume, watch the twinkling lights dance across her features. "I bet it looks beautiful."

She nodded. Then turned back to the scraggly pine and caught another handful of needles. "So much work, just for one day."

"Most people would think it's worth the effort. Don't you?"

"Some days, yes. Some days…" She took a breath. "You asked me a couple days ago about my mother and Christmas."

"I'm sorry. I shouldn't have. I know it's a difficult subject." Livia hadn't told him much about her childhood, just that her mother had walked out on her children while they were young and never come back. When her father didn't step into the parental role, Livia stepped up and raised her younger sister.

He hadn't shared much, if anything, about his own childhood, and yet curiosity to know more about her burned in his chest.

"And then tonight," she went on, "when you said what you did—"

"I'm sorry. I didn't mean any of it." Regret weighed inside him.

"No, you were right, Edward. I keep telling myself that you're wrong, but you're not. I am trying to force you into this little perfect family because ever since that baby was born, all I've ever wanted is to give Piper what I never had."

"Livia—"

She put up a hand. "Let me…let me tell you about Christmas at my house. And then maybe you'll understand a little more."

"Okay."

The pine needles coursed across her palm, and Livia watched for a moment as they tumbled end over end. "When I was a little girl, Christmas was always my dad's thing. It was like he was trying so hard to make it perfect, to make her happy. But my mom would complain about the mess, complain about the extra chores of decorating. So my dad would be the one to get the tree out of the attic. We had a plastic one. Less mess, you know? Anyway, Melody and I would help him set it up, and though we fought over putting on the star, we each had our favorite ornaments to hang. There weren't very many. My mom thought they were a waste of money, but the ones we did have, the three of us would hang." She tipped her palm and the needles spilled onto the pavement. "That was all we ever had. A tree. No stockings or cookie jar Santas. Just the tree. But when you're little, it's enough."

"Nothing else?" He'd grown up in this town, where Christmas was practically considered a sport. Decorations had been—and still were—a friendly neighborhood competition.

She shook her head. "It was a battle just to get that

tree, believe me. I always wondered about that. About why my mother didn't like Christmas."

He'd never known a mother who didn't celebrate holidays with an all-out effort. His own mother had been the driving force behind Christmas when he'd been little. But then after Katie died—

He cut that thought off right in its tracks.

"Why do you think she felt that way?" he asked.

Livia thought for a long moment, her face turned to the moonlit sky. Clouds drifted across the full moon, causing it to drop a gauzy light over the town, a glow over her features. "I think it just reminded her of the box she was in. All those holiday family gatherings and family activities, and most of all, family expectations. I think she always felt trapped by being a mother."

"And that's why you think she left?" he asked the question with a gentle touch, almost afraid to push her down the dark corridor she hated, but sensing she needed to talk about this. Livia clutched those pine needles like they might escape, the same tight way she held on to her emotions. Pot calling the kettle black, he thought, because he did the same thing. "Is that why, Liv?"

Livia nodded. Tears glistened in her eyes and her face crumpled, as if the last brick in her emotional wall had been removed. "Was it really too much to ask?" she asked, her voice small and shredded. "To have a cookie jar Santa?"

His heart broke for her. For the years without stockings and cookie jar Santas and most of all, without a mother. For Livia Perkins, the holiday wasn't about decorations or a Christmas ham. It was about the absence of a mother who loved and cherished her family. About growing up in charge of everything. Poor Livia, trying so hard all her life to fill shoes she didn't fit.

He drew her to him and cradled her head against his chest. She hesitated only a second, then curved into him, and he pressed a kiss to her forehead. "No, Livia, it's not too much. Not at all."

She turned toward him, her face still filled with doubt. He pressed another kiss to her forehead, then a second further down, along her nose. Then she tipped up higher, and his lips came down a third time and met hers.

Kissing Livia was like coming home. Connection arced inside him, the kind of connection that came with someone who knew you better than you knew yourself. She tasted of everything that had ever been sweet and good in his life.

She let out a soft mew, and any noble intentions he might have had disappeared with that sound. He crushed Livia's body against his, hands roaming down her back, wanting as much of her as he could have. Her breasts pressed against his chest, and his body reacted, an erection rising hard and fast, pulse throbbing in his head, demanding more.

But he reined in his desire. Now was not the time, nor the place. And he already knew where caving to his desires got him—in bed with Livia and considering the kind of future he knew he couldn't have. She deserved a man who gave her his whole heart.

So he drew back, but didn't let her go. Not quite yet. "I'm sorry. I..." He let out a gust. "You know what, I'm not sorry. I'm glad I kissed you."

"You're...glad?"

"I've been wanting to kiss you again ever since the other day." Damn, why did he keep complicating this? "I've thought about almost nothing else. I have missed kissing you, Livia."

She tried to hold back a smile, but it burst on her face like a sunrise. "I've missed kissing you, too."

"Then we should do more of that." He danced another kiss along her lips. He wanted to hold onto this moment. To capture the happiness he felt, bottle it up and save it for those dark lonely days ahead. "A lot more."

Her smile held, then fell, a little at a time. "Why?"

"What do you mean, why? Because it feels good." He leaned in to kiss her again, but she put up a hand and stopped him.

"But where's it going to go? To a relationship? To marriage?"

The cold hard reality of their situation thrust itself between them. The happiness he'd been trying so hard to grasp flitted into the ether.

"I'm not made for that, Livia."

"Why not? Because it's hard to open up? To build a relationship? You think it's easy for me? I don't want to spin my wheels and end up in the same place as we did a year ago. I want more now."

"More?"

"A *real* marriage, Edward. The kind where we're both madly in love with each other, and we're building a happy family. You of all people should understand why that's important to me after what I just told you. I don't want your money, I don't want Piper and me to be your 'responsibility.' I want you to be here, to be with us—" on the last word, her voice broke "—because you love us and can't imagine life without me and our daughter."

He released her and stepped away. She didn't understand what she was asking of him, and why he couldn't give it to her. It wasn't a matter of not wanting that dream—it was a matter of not being the kind of man to fulfill it. Hell, he'd never learned how to be that kind of man. Why did Livia keep thinking he could magically change? "Why does it have to be all or nothing with you, Livia?"

"Because I deserve it all, Edward. And so does Piper." She moved forward, put a soft hand on his shoulder. "And so do you."

CHAPTER EIGHT

"Snow today, that's the word." Ray settled into the kitchen chair opposite his son with a mug of coffee and a handful of cookies. Sugar Santa cookies, with sprinklings of red sugar. Probably came from Samantha MacGregor's bakery, and most likely delivered by Sam herself, who'd already sent over a basket of carrot and bran muffins. "About darn time. It's not Christmas without a little snow."

"Since when did you get the Christmas spirit? You got the tree, the cookies. Heck, I half expect you to start wearing reindeer antlers."

"No antlers. I ain't going that far." Ray chuckled, then shrugged. "I dunno. I guess it's only been the last couple weeks or so. Nothing like a little heart attack wake-up call. I realized I've been missing out all these years. On you, on Christmas trees, you name it. Working too hard and taking care too little. Your mother always did all that stuff and when she was gone—" Ray sighed.

Edward nodded. "I know. It wasn't the same." And it had been a hard road to build a relationship with his father that extended beyond small talk. Living together had forced them to talk, though, which was probably a good thing.

"Caroline, God rest her soul, was the heart of this

family." Ray glanced out the window, his eyes misting. "There are days when I miss her so much, it's hard to breathe."

Edward saw the deep love in his father's eyes, still strong after all these years, and envied the emotion. "What's it like? To love someone that much that they're…almost a part of your soul?"

A smile stole across his father's face. "It's like becoming more of who you are. It's like the other person brings out the best in you and makes you want to be even better. I tell ya, I was never half as good a person as Caroline. But I tried." Ray crossed his hands on the table. "I sure wish I'd learned that lesson sooner, while she was still here and we could have had something… more. I always thought if I worked hard and provided well, I'd show her how much I cared. I guess I didn't realize until the end that all she ever wanted was for me to be here."

Edward nodded. His mother had sat at this very kitchen table on hundreds of nights waiting for Ray to come home from work. After Katie had died, it was as if his mother needed Ray to be around even more, to hold together the three parts remaining in her family. "She loved you, Dad."

"I know. And I didn't know what a hell of a gift that was until it was gone." His gaze returned to his son's.

"You never told me."

"I'm not much for talking. Never was, and after Katie died—" Pain creased Ray's features. "I just thought it'd be easier not to talk at all."

Edward nodded. "Me, too."

The two men exchanged a glance. They'd become each other's emotional twins in many ways. "Not the smartest thing I could have done. Your mother needed me you needed me, and I was…"

"Not there."

"Yeah. Sorry."

"It's okay, Dad."

Ray let out a cough, clearly still a little uncomfortable with the hard talk. "Anyway, when you find love, you hold on tight. You do whatever it takes to make it work. Because believe me, that kind of love doesn't come along every day."

Edward twirled his coffee cup in his hands. "I don't know if I'm wired that way."

"You are. You just don't like to flip that emotional switch. I know, I'm the same way. It was hard for me to become a man who talked about what he thought, how he felt. I had to learn, because I didn't want to miss one more day, not when I came so close to…" He shuddered. "Anyway, that didn't happen. Sometimes, son, you gotta open your heart to see what's on the other side."

"Kinda like having open-heart surgery?"

Ray laughed. "Yeah, kinda."

They sat quiet for a while, two men sharing memories of a woman they had both loved dearly. Edward digested his father's advice. Maybe his father was right—or maybe he was just thinking his son could be more than he really was. Then again, Ray had changed, albeit very late in life. Was there still time for Edward to learn a new way of connecting?

He rose, refilled his coffee, and leaned back against the counter. He'd enjoyed these quiet days with his father. After all this was over, Edward vowed to spend more time here in this bright kitchen in Riverbend.

Ray got to his feet, then leaned against the counter beside his son. "Now when am I going to meet this grandchild of mine?"

"Meet her?"

"You didn't think I'd let her first Christmas go by without at least a howdy-do? I even got her a gift."

"You bought Piper a gift?" His father was full of surprises today. "How? When?"

"Soon as you told me about her. I can use the internet as easily as anyone else, and wouldn't you know, they'll ship your items lickety-split." Ray snapped his fingers. "Amazing, that Internet."

Edward leaned back and studied the man he used to think he knew as well as himself. "You surprise me, Dad."

"Good. I meant to. I wasn't the best father for you, but I can change that with this little baby. And so can you."

"I just found out about her a few days ago. I haven't even had time to be a father."

Ray waved that off. "I don't care if you found out three days or three years ago. It's never too late to be a good father. At least that's my new motto."

"I don't know, Dad." Edward turned to the sink. He started the water and added soap to wash the few dishes from breakfast. True, Ray had changed a lot since his heart attack, but it was a whole lot different to build a relationship with another adult than to care for a baby. A baby who would grow to depend on Edward to be there, forever and ever. Once he stepped into that quagmire, he knew getting out wouldn't be that easy.

"You know what the right thing is to do. Problem is, you're just too damned scared to do it."

"I'm not scared." Edward rinsed a glass, then set it in the strainer to dry.

"Okay, then prove it." Ray laid a hand on Edward's shoulder, a firm grip that said he was serious about the invitation. "Dinner is at five. I expect to see my new granddaughter and her mother here at the kitchen table."

Christmas Eve.

Livia sat in a rocking chair by the window in Piper's nursery, her daughter on her lap, while Piper sucked down her second bottle of the day. The rest of the morning stretched ahead of Livia, more or less empty of responsibilities.

There was the house to clean, of course. And Piper to feed, dress and bathe. But no shift at the tree lot, no plans for the evening except possibly taking Piper to the Winterfest. All the presents had been bought and wrapped and stowed under the tree. A ham sat in the refrigerator, waiting for Christmas dinner. Tonight, she planned on ordering pizza—Melody's favorite meal, and a concession Livia had made for the holiday.

She'd called her father first thing this morning and when he said he wouldn't make it to Riverbend for Christmas, she promised to fly out there with Piper after the holiday was over. He'd seemed reluctant to have the company, saying he had work to do, but she'd insisted. If she could convince Melody to go along too, maybe they'd have a true family holiday. One way or another, she was going to build this family and keep it together. For Piper's sake, if nothing else.

Piper looked up at her mother as she drank, her blue eyes wide and seeming to ask questions Livia had no answers to. Like what she was going to do about Edward.

Edward.

Livia's fingers went to her lips, tracing where he had kissed her. The man knew how to kiss, that was for sure.

It was keeping a relationship together that he had trouble with. The problem was, a large part of her still cared about him and still hoped for the impossible. It was as if she'd had a taste of something delicious and couldn't accept that the recipe was a temporary one.

"Oh, baby," she whispered to Piper, "half of me hopes he moves to Costa Rica. The other half hopes he stays right here." Piper didn't have an opinion on anything other than her bottle.

Down the hall, she heard the soft chime of the doorbell. "Melody?" Livia called down. "Can you get that? I'm feeding Piper."

"Okay," Melody answered. The door opened, then there was the sound of Melody greeting someone. Probably Earl, who had said he was going to stop by today with a thank-you gift for working the tree lot. She'd told him he didn't need to thank her, but he'd insisted.

"Piper's almost done," Livia called to her sister. "Tell Earl I'll be there in a few minutes."

Footsteps sounded in the hall. A second later, the nursery door nudged open and Edward, not Melody, not Earl, stepped into the nursery. "Your sister said you were in here."

Every time she saw Edward, it was like seeing him again for the first time. She forced herself to maintain a neutral face, to not betray her hurt and disappointment that he hadn't changed, that he still wanted a relationship with about as much depth as a puddle.

This was the future, she told herself. Edward stopping by from time to time, to see their child. It wouldn't be the traditional family environment she'd dreamed of, but it would be enough. It would have to be.

"Sorry. It's feeding time at the zoo." Livia smiled,

then gave Piper's head a gentle rub. "I'm almost done if you want to wait—"

"I'm fine. I can talk to you here." He leaned against the doorjamb.

Livia adjusted her arm under Piper's head, then repositioned the bottle. "So what did you come by for?"

"My father is inviting you to Christmas Eve dinner at his house."

"Your father? The man who never cooked." She raised a dubious brow. She'd met Raymond Graham a few times and had instantly liked the cantankerous softie. He'd made it clear one time that cooking was something he didn't believe in doing, "not when there's a perfectly good pizza shop in town that delivers," as he'd said.

"I didn't say it would be good. I just said he invited you, your sister, and…" Edward let out a breath, "his granddaughter."

It wasn't the words *my daughter* or even Piper's name, but it was a step forward from *the child.* Maybe someday down the road they'd progress to Edward having an actual relationship with his daughter. That would be enough, Livia reminded herself.

Even if she didn't believe it, even if it hurt to think of seeing him all the time and not being with him. How on earth was she going to sit across a dinner table from him tonight?

She'd find a way. Piper came first, and everything else, including Livia's broken heart, came second. "Sure, that sounds great. Can I bring anything?"

"I…don't know. I'll ask him. I'm kind of new at this company-for-dinner thing myself."

"I remember." The words escaped her in a quiet rush. When she and Edward had been dating last year, his kitchen had been as bare as an empty box. They usually either ate at restaurants or brought home extras from the banquet hall. The one time he'd invited her for dinner at his house, he'd forgotten to shop for the meal and ended up calling down to Rustica and ordering a delivered meal. "You are great at ordering takeout, though."

He chuckled. "We all have our skills in life."

"We do indeed." She glanced down at Piper. "What's your skill going to be, baby girl? President? Nuclear physicist? Pianist?" Piper, of course, didn't answer, but Livia didn't care. She just marveled at her child, and the peaceful look on her face as she finished her meal. "This is my favorite time of day, when I feed her. It's just a few minutes of the two of us being quiet. It makes me slow down, focus on nothing but Piper. It may sound silly, but it really helps me focus on what's important."

Edward watched them for a long moment, then he came a little further into the room. He seemed hesitant, unsure if he was even invited. "Do you think…maybe I can do it?"

It took a second before Livia realized Edward was asking to feed Piper. She tried not to get her hopes up, but they rose all the same. She stood, keeping Piper's bottle still in her mouth, and vacated the rocking chair. "Sure. Have a seat and I'll put her in your arms."

His big frame seemed to dwarf the delicate white chair, but he settled into it without complaint. "Now what?"

"Put out your arms." When he did, she leaned forward, and gently placed Piper in his arms. At first, Edward sat stiff, Piper again lying like a log on his forearms. Livia couldn't help but laugh. "Relax. She doesn't bite." Livia eased the baby back against Edward's chest, settling Piper into the nook of his arms, then she reached for Edward's right hand, and placed it on top of the bottle. "Just keep that right there, and you'll have a happy little girl."

He shifted but didn't bring Piper a whole lot closer to him, as if he was afraid to get too near the baby. "Doesn't she need to burp or…breathe or something?"

Livia chuckled. "Burping is at the end, and she breathes while she drinks. Watch."

Edward leaned down and watched as Piper paused in drinking. Her nostrils flared with an inhale, then she started drinking again after the exhale. She repeated the action over and over, as the formula level dropped more and more inside the bottle. As the bottle drained, Edward seemed to relax and shifted Piper a tiny bit closer. "Wow. She's got it down to a science."

"Yup. A genius already."

Edward's gaze swept over Livia's features, and a smile curved across his face. "I love the way you look at her."

"The way I look at Piper?"

"You just…love her so much. And it shows."

Livia trailed a finger along Piper's cheek. "She's easy to love. I loved her before she was born, but love her more every day I spend with her."

"But don't you worry that you'll—" he looked down at the baby and then his demeanor tightened again "—let her down?"

"Of course I do. I worry about that every day. But all I can do is my best." Livia shrugged.

Piper had finished the bottle and Edward took it out of her mouth and set it on the end table. The baby lay in his arms, blinking up at him, as if wondering who the new chef was. "What if your best isn't good enough?"

"I don't think about that, Edward. I worry about what

I feed her. I worry about keeping her dry and warm. I worry about keeping the house clean and as germ-free as possible. But I don't worry about things that could be dozens of years away. Filling my head with what-ifs only distracts me from the most important thing."

"And what's that?"

She knelt down beside him and the baby. "Loving her. That's the easiest thing to do. And the most important. Don't you agree?"

He didn't answer. As if on cue, Piper started to squirm. Edward held the baby toward Livia. "I think she needs to be burped or something."

"You can do it, if you want. It's not all that hard."

Doubt filled his eyes, and he looked about ready to bolt from the room. Feeding had been easy, because Piper had just lain there and done all the work. But burping was a more involved, hands-on job, and Edward looked about as comfortable with that idea as a bull walking across thin ice. "I...I don't want to screw it up."

Livia's first instinct was to take Piper and make this easier on Edward. To take control of the situation, something Melody accused her of all the time. But in the long run, that hadn't gotten the results Livia wanted, had it? She'd allowed Edward to have the distance he wanted, rather than letting him just...deal. Like she had from the day she'd found out she was pregnant. If she had called him that day and told him about the baby on the way, would he be as awkward around her as he was? Would he have had more time to warm to the idea, maybe even look forward to the baby's arrival? Or would he have remained the same closed-emotions man she'd met last year?

She propped a fist on her hip. "Are you telling me the man who has successfully built a banquet hall into a national venues company is afraid to burp a fourteen-pound baby?"

"This is different. She's living, breathing…I could hurt her."

She nearly laughed at the worry in big, strong Edward's face. She'd never seen a man look more uncomfortable and unsure of himself. Edward, too, of all people, who had impressed her from the start with his command of his company and of a room. He'd been confident, charming, sure of everything.

Apparently sure of everything but babies.

"I'm right here, Edward. You can do it." She pressed his hands upward, guiding Piper into place against his shoulder. She felt him stiffen when the baby made contact. "It's okay. You won't hurt her. Now, rub her back in a circle, then pat."

He did as Livia instructed, but with a feather touch. "Like this?"

"A little harder. You gotta work that air out of her. Don't worry. You won't break her."

He patted more firmly and in seconds, was rewarded with a very loud, very long belch. "Holy cow. She did that?"

"Yep. Takes after her daddy that way." She tossed him a teasing grin.

"Hey." But then Edward's face softened, and he turned to peek at Piper. "You got quite a set of lungs on you, kid."

Piper reached up a chubby little fist, and grabbed Edward's nose. She tugged at him, holding tight with tiny fingers to the prominent feature. Piper's eyes widened, and she stared at Edward, not moving, not making a sound, as if she were memorizing him.

For a moment, Edward's gaze locked on Piper's too.

The two of them, so similar in features, looking like mirror images of each other. Then Piper let out a squeal, and a little joyous bounce. Livia knew that look—Piper was happy.

Edward shifted his nose out of her grasp. "Uh…I think she's done eating. You want to take her?"

Livia nodded, trying not to be disappointed that Edward had abdicated so quickly. She took the baby, then got to her feet. "Thanks."

"Yeah, no problem." He got out of the chair and gestured toward it. "All yours again."

"I'd love to sit down, but it's time to get dressed and start our day." She crossed to the changing table, laid Piper down, and reached for a new diaper. Under Livia's watchful hand, Piper kicked and gurgled, reaching toward the mobile hanging over her head.

Edward lingered by the door, as if he didn't want to leave yet. "You did a nice job decorating for Christmas. Wait till you see my father's tree. It's pretty pitiful. But in our defense, it was decorated by two guys."

Livia laughed. She finished putting on Piper's diaper and helped the baby wriggle out of her pajamas. "I don't care. And Piper won't notice at all."

Edward still hung just inside the room, and Livia got the sense that he was working up to saying something. She busied herself with dressing Piper in a clean onesie, then a bright red sweat suit with a fuzzy Santa head on the front. It wasn't until Livia was sliding thick white socks onto Piper's feet that Edward finally spoke.

"When I was a kid, Christmas was a big family thing," he said, his gaze on Piper, but Livia sensed he wasn't really seeing anything. "My mom loved Christmas, and she made sure every single holiday was a production. Or at least, she used to."

Piper was all dressed, so Livia picked her up and held her to her chest. She wondered why Edward was still here. Why he kept saying one thing and doing another. It was as if everything inside him was a conflict. As much as her head told her to run away, that he was only going to shut her out again, and she should end the torture of seeing him, her heart told her to give him one more chance. Because the man she'd glimpsed a couple times this week was in there, somewhere. "I bet that was nice."

He nodded. "I was in charge of hanging the ornaments and my sister was in charge of the tinsel. They still had tinsel in those days. Godawful mess it made, but my mother loved it. She said it gave the tree sparkle."

"I didn't know you had a sister."

He swallowed hard and looked toward the wall. "I don't talk about her much."

And then Livia knew. The pieces began to come together. "Is she…the Piper you mentioned?"

He nodded and his eyes glistened with unshed tears. "She was a talker from the day she born. My mom would say, 'Katie-girl, you're always piping up about something or other.' And that's how she got the nickname."

"I had no idea. I'm sorry. I—"

"No, it's perfect. I'm honored, actually, that you would do that." His gaze lit on his sister's namesake for a moment. "It means more to me than you can know."

"I'm glad, then. And if our little girl's vocal abilities are any indication, I think she's going to grow into that name quite well."

A smile flitted across his face. "I agree."

"So why did you never tell me you had a sister?"

Edward didn't answer the question. Not directly, anyway. He ran a hand down the string of the mobile hanging over the changing table, capturing the little zebra at the end and letting it bounce against his palm. "When she was six, Katie was starting to doubt Santa. I think one of the kids at school said something to her and she came home, all upset. Anyway, that year, she wanted proof that Santa existed. She wrote him a long letter, mailed it herself, and wouldn't tell any of us what she wrote in there or what she asked for."

"I bet lots of kids have done the same thing." Livia swayed a little with Piper, hoping to keep the baby happy long enough for Edward to finish his story. She knew, in that intuitive sense of someone who has been close to another person, that telling it was important. To him, and maybe to closing a long-open wound. "What happened at Christmas if no one saw the letter?"

"Well, she let it slip to me one day what she really wanted. A red bicycle. Bright red with a white seat." He chuckled softly at the memory but Livia could hear the raw edge in that laugh. "That was what she had her heart set on, and she told me if she got it, then she'd know Santa was real." He crossed to the window, looking out at the bleak, gray landscape. The promised snow had yet to start falling and the entire town seemed caught in a dreary bubble of anticipation. "I told my mom, and of course, she went right out and bought a bicycle. Katie was overjoyed on Christmas morning, and the first thing she did when she saw that bike was hug me. It was like our special secret, that Santa was real."

"Edward, that's so sweet."

"We were typical siblings. Rarely got along. Didn't hug much, if ever. So that one hug was a big deal, I just didn't know how big at the time. God, I wish I had." He paused, took in a long breath. "I really wish I had known."

"Known what?"

He leaned a palm on the cold glass, spreading his fingers against the bleak view. "That it was the last hug I'd ever receive from her. I guess I never realized how much I loved my little sister until—"

The room in the air stilled. Livia caught her breath.

"—until she wasn't there anymore," he finished. His voice cracked.

"Not...not there anymore?"

He nodded, and it seemed like his shoulders dropped under an invisible weight. "Katie, oh, she was my shadow. Everywhere I went, she had to go, too. Drove me out my mind. I was a boy, I had boy things to do. And the worst thing you can have is your little sister tagging along."

Livia glanced at Piper and wondered if there would ever be a sibling to tag along with her. Someone to fight over toys with, someone to hug when a thunderstorm crashed overhead, someone to spill secrets to and share cookies with. As much as Melody sometimes drove her crazy, Livia was glad to have her sister.

"It was Christmas break," Edward went on, his voice softer now, lost in a day decades past, "and I was going to play in the woods behind our house with my friends. We had it in our heads to build a snow fort." He pivoted toward her. "Crazy things kids do when they're bored, you know?"

She nodded. Didn't speak.

He turned back to the window, seeing, she was sure, another wintry day. A day off from school, filled with the kind of empty agenda children enjoyed every day. The world bright and limitless. Edward, totally unaware of the shadows lurking around the corner.

"Katie wanted to tag along," he said. "I complained,

tried to talk Katie into staying home, but she really wanted to be with the 'big boys,' as she used to call us. The last thing my mother said before we left was…" His voice trailed off, then he took in a deep breath, and tried again. "The last thing she said was, *'Watch out for Katie.'*" Those last four words seemed to rip from his throat. He shuddered out a long breath and grabbed at the windowsill with both hands, pressing his forehead to the cold glass. "Watch out for Katie. And I couldn't even do that." The words were a sob, not a sentence.

Livia crossed to Edward and laid a gentle hand on his shoulder. He tensed, then relaxed, but didn't turn toward her. She almost didn't want to press this, to ask anything more, because this was clearly a hurt that reached deep inside his soul, but she also knew that letting this fester even one more day was no good for Edward. "Tell me what happened."

Long moments passed. Cars went by on the street outside, the microwave let out a series of beeps, and Piper squirmed a little in Livia's arms. When Edward spoke again, his voice was hushed and hoarse.

"She…she fell, right over the edge and into a ravine. It was snowy and icy, and we were hurrying through the woods, and she was struggling to keep up because it was hilly and slippery, but all I wanted to do was lose her, because I didn't want her tagging along. And then she fell, and all I heard was her calling for me—*Edward, Edward*—and I thought she just wanted me to wait up, and I didn't want to do that, because I was annoyed she was even there." The words spilled from him in a rush. "So I kept going. And going. And by the time I realized she wasn't behind me anymore—" He cut off the sentence, and his eyes welled. "It…it was too late. I couldn't do anything. I tried, but I couldn't get her out of there. I couldn't save her." Now he turned to face Livia, his face crumpled with regret. "I tried, Livia, I tried so hard."

"Oh, Edward, you were only seven. What could you do?" She could imagine the scene. The boys, tromping through the woods, laughing, joking, and then the realization that one person was missing. Returning through the woods, calling Katie's name, and then…seeing her crumpled at the bottom of a ravine.

All the pieces finally fell into place. Edward's considerable guilt over an accidental fire, and another hurt girl. His refusal to have children, to get close to them. To even consider being a parent. "All these years, you carried this guilt with you for something that was an accident," she said. "Edward, you were a child yourself. Nobody could expect you to see this coming, to prevent it, or to save her."

He shook his head again, stronger this time. "That's no excuse."

"I'm not saying it's an excuse. It's a reality. You were a little boy. Annoyed with his little sister. Every boy in the world has felt that way at least a hundred times."

Edward spun around and in his eyes, she saw the intolerable weight of his regrets. *"I didn't stop,"* he said, the words slow and sharp, like lashes against his back. "I could have saved her, Livia. Don't you understand that? It was my fault. Mine. And my mother was never the same after that day. She died because she never found happiness again after Katie died. I did that, Livia. *I* did that."

"Oh, Edward." Her heart broke for him, and she wished he could see himself the way she saw him. A man who tried his best, day after day, and still couldn't escape the weight of his past. "You've always been the strong one. Maybe too strong. You take the world on your shoulders when it has plenty of other people to help carry the load." She reached up and cupped his cheek and waited until his eyes connected with hers. "You made a simple, understandable choice. More than twenty years ago. Surely you don't blame—"

"Yes, I can keep blaming myself, Livia. Don't you see? I'm no good watching over other people. Katie, Miranda..." His voice trailed off and his face shattered when he took in their child, now asleep on Livia's shoulders. "Piper."

"There are no guarantees in this life, Edward. All you do is the best you can."

"But what if my best isn't good enough? What if she gets hurt, too?" He shook his head, and looked away, as if merely the sight of Piper's innocent, cherubic face undid him.

"You'll never know unless you try." She shifted closer to him, turning until he could see Piper's sleepy face.

But he moved away, putting distance between himself and his child, and most of all, between himself and Livia. "I'm sorry. I can't take that chance."

She watched him standing in the shadows of the nursery, a broken man who had kept all this pain to himself for so long. He had a chance now to have everything and he was throwing it away. Closing the door between them. Again.

She reached down and took his hand. She gripped his palm firmly, trying to tell him with her touch how much she believed in Edward Graham. "Come with me."

"Where are we going?"

"To make amends." She smiled up at him. "And maybe then, you'll realize that doing the best you can is the only thing you can do."

CHAPTER NINE

EDWARD had gone along with Livia's mysterious plan for the first hour, mainly because she wouldn't answer any questions and wouldn't tell him what they were doing at a superstore about five miles outside of Riverbend. He'd pushed the cart while she loaded it, wondering about the purchases. They didn't buy much, mostly a laptop computer. For Piper? He didn't understand it, and Livia wasn't talking.

It wasn't that he couldn't afford it—Edward's company had done very, very well and money was not a problem for him—it was that he wasn't used to being in the passenger's seat. He wondered if perhaps Livia was keeping him in the dark on purpose, to get him to loosen the reins a little on his life.

Truth be told, he felt drained, empty, after telling Livia about Katie. Her unwavering support of him filled him, and for the first time since his little sister died, Edward began to feel the bonds of that self-created prison begin to ease. He had opened his heart, let Livia peek inside...and it had all been okay. Maybe he could change.

And in the end, maybe find...

Peace.

And boy, did he need that.

"Who is all this for?" he asked after they had loaded their purchases into the back of her car, then settled Piper inside and got in themselves.

"You'll see." She put her car in gear and pulled out of the store parking lot. The sky above was still gray, not so much as a single flake of the predicted snow. Didn't look like the storm was ever going to make an appearance.

"Livia, I'd really like to know what the plan is."

She laughed. "This drives you crazy, doesn't it?"

"What?"

"Not being in control. The boss had to hand over control to someone else for a change."

"I've already done that," he said. "My vice president is in charge of my company right now."

She snorted. "Uh-huh. And how in charge is he?"

"What do you mean?"

"I mean, did you step back, hands-off entirely, or is he following your directions to the T? Doing everything the Edward Graham way?" She eyed him before returning her attention to the road.

"Well, it's important that there's a cohesiveness to the leadership and—"

"Just as I thought." She turned to him and grinned. "We are two of a kind, Edward. Two control freaks who can't let other people be in charge."

"I let you drive today." He pointed to the steering wheel. He didn't add that there hadn't been much choice in that arena, considering Livia had a car seat and he didn't.

She chuckled. "And how many times did you try to give me directions? Even though you didn't even know where we were going."

He smiled. He'd been caught—nailed to a board with

precision by Livia. Sometimes he wondered if anyone knew him as well as this woman. She'd been right about everything—about his inability to give up control, about his vice president following precisely in Edward's footsteps. Hell, he hadn't even been able to sign the documents to sell the company yet. All this talk of moving forward and getting out from under the yoke of CEO, and he hadn't really taken one step in that direction. Maybe that was part of it, too—the tighter he held the reins, the less risk he had to take. Was he doing the same thing with his heart? With Livia? "I was trying to guess what you were up to."

"And were you right?"

He laughed, and thought of where they'd ended up. He'd expected a restaurant. Maybe a trip to a baby store to load up Piper with enough clothes for the next seven years. "Not even close."

"Good." A self-satisfied smile curved across her face.

"You look like a cat that caught a mouse."

She laughed, and he realized how much he had missed her laugh. She had a melodic, sweet voice, and when Livia laughed, it was like putting notes to that music. "Not quite."

"So are you going to at least tell me why we are doing this mystery thing we're doing?"

"For you to get past the panic stage."

"The what?"

She turned right, heading back into Riverbend. "Before I had Piper, I'd wake up all the time in the middle of the night, worried to death about everything. From whether I could provide for her to whether I'd remember to change her diaper. I was a wreck by the time I had her, so sure I'd screw up something. But you know what a baby teaches you pretty quickly?"

He shook his head.

"The minute that baby arrives, it's sink or swim. And really, even when you sink—" she paused at a stop sign and glanced at Piper in the rearview mirror "—like the time I cut her finger when I was trying to trim her nails, then bumped her head on the shelf hurrying to get her finger under some cold water, sometimes you learn that you can handle it. That in the end, it'll all work out fine. That worrying about the what-ifs did nothing but waste time."

He sobered. The light mood of the morning had disappeared. "Sometimes those what-ifs come true."

"And sometimes the results weren't nearly as disastrous as you suspected." She took a right, then stopped the car in front of a small two-story Cape-style house.

His blood froze. He saw now why Livia had driven. If he'd been behind the wheel, he never would have turned down this street, much less stopped at this house. What was Livia thinking? This wasn't going to make anything better. "Why are we here?"

"Because it's time, Edward." She laid a hand over his. "It's time."

She was right. But that didn't mean he liked the fact. He wanted nothing more than to stay in this car and not go inside that house. But where had avoidance gotten him in the last year? Nowhere good, that was for sure. Instead of moving on, he'd been wallowing in regrets. And in doing so, in thinking he was best at working through this on his own, he'd once lost the best woman he'd ever met, driving her and his child away.

If he didn't do this, he knew—knew as well as he knew his own name—that his past would keep on being the biggest obstacle to his future. A future that he was beginning to hope would always include Livia.

"Okay." He reached for the door handle and got out of Livia's car.

She got out too, then retrieved Piper from her car seat in the back. She slung the diaper bag over one shoulder, then stepped onto the sidewalk beside Edward. Her smaller hand slipped into his. He squeezed her fingers. "If I forget to tell you later…thank you."

Livia turned a smile on him. "You're welcome."

He nodded, then took a step forward. And another. A crisp winter wind blew against him, but he kept going forward.

Until he reached Miranda Willett's front step. And finally faced what he'd done his best to avoid for nearly a year.

The door opened before they pushed the bell. "What the hell are you doing here?" Richard Willett's face held a stone-cold anger.

"I came by to deliver a long overdue apology," Edward said. "Very long overdue."

The anger ebbed a little in Richard's face. He stood in the doorway, hesitating. Finally, he let out a long breath, like releasing air from a balloon, and stepped back to allow Edward and Livia entry. "Come in, then."

They stepped inside a bright, warm home. The walls were covered in soft shades of blue and white. White Christmas lights swagged the archway between the living room and dining room, then cascaded down the staircase. And in the corner stood the scraggly pine tree from the tree lot. Livia was surprised to see it covered in ornaments, so many she was sure the tree would topple from the weight.

Alicia Willett had been sitting in a chair by the window, a newspaper on her lap. She rose, then crossed to

Edward and Livia. She followed Livia's gaze. "The tree looks beautiful, doesn't it?"

"Yes. It does. A big improvement over how it looked in the lot, too."

"Miranda tends to go a little crazy at Christmas. She puts Mrs. Claus to shame. And even though she insisted she didn't want a tree—didn't want a Christmas at all, in fact—as soon as we got it set up, she had her dad get the ornaments out of the attic and insisted we hang them up together. Every last one." A tender look filled Alicia's eyes. She stood by the tree and fingered a hand-made gingerbread man. "Miranda's been making ornaments for as long as I can remember. When we look at this tree, it's like seeing her grow up all over again."

Edward cleared his throat. "Can I speak to her?"

The Willetts looked at each other, their faces filled with the protective caution of parents. It was a look Livia knew well. If she could have created a giant bubble to cushion Piper for the rest of her life, she would have.

Finally, Miranda's mother nodded. "Okay. I think that will be all right."

Richard tensed. "I don't want to upset her."

"Richard, we have to let her go sometime. She's a big girl. As she reminds us all the time. She can handle this."

"Follow me." Richard headed up the staircase, with Edward on his heels, and Livia bringing up the rear. From her perch on Livia's hip, Piper looked around, wide-eyed at the new surroundings.

Richard stopped halfway up and turned to face them. "Do you have any idea what my daughter's been through?" He didn't wait for an answer. "Six surgeries. Four skin grafts. And down the road, more surgeries as the scar tissues contract. She wears a pressure suit on half her body for twenty-three hours a day. And the pain—" Richard cursed and shook his head. "It's been a nightmare. The medical bills are astronomical, I'm sure. But someone paid—" He cut off his sentence and stared at Edward, pieces clicking together. "You?"

"It was the least I could do."

Richard considered Edward for a long time. A hundred emotions washed over his face, as he realized the man he'd been blaming all these months had been the one footing hundreds of thousands in medical bills. "Well, thank you. We'll pay you back—"

Edward put up a hand. "I don't want your money. I'll pay for her care for as long as she needs it. Whatever she needs."

"Thank you." Richard's voice was gruff. He turned and continued up the stairs. They stopped at the top of the stairs, then Richard knocked on the first door on the right. "Miranda, you have company."

There was a muffled okay from the other side, then Richard turned the knob and opened the door. He stepped inside the room first, then turned to allow Edward and Livia to enter.

The first thing Livia noticed was the album covers. Some faded, some dog-eared, some as pristine as the day they were printed. It has been years since she'd seen actual LPs, but Miranda was apparently a fan of rock music and the artistic LP covers created years ago. Instead of wallpaper, she had all the classics lining her walls—the Rolling Stones, The Beatles, Led Zeppelin. An ancient computer sat on a small desk by her bedside, along with a stack of books on graphic design and music magazines. Classic rock played loud on the stereo on the bookcase, shivering the Christmas lights hung from corner to corner of the ceiling.

Miranda sat in the center of a double bed, propped up by a half-dozen fluffy white pillows. A thick white comforter covered part of her legs, but not enough to block the view of the pressure suit compressing the bottom half of her body. Long tubular bandages covered her arms. Her hair was cut in a short, boyish style, but Livia could still see the bald patches where her scalp had burned. Her face had been mostly spared, thank God, except for a few patches marked by unnaturally white blotches.

No wonder Edward hadn't wanted to come. For a second, Livia considered leaving, but they were here now, and it was, as she'd said, far past time Edward dealt with his demons.

Richard thumbed down the volume on the stereo. "I'll let you all talk." Then he left the room, giving his daughter one last concerned glance.

"Hey, Mr. Graham." Miranda smiled, and it seemed to transform her face from scarred to beautiful. "What are you doing here?"

"I wanted to see how you were doing. And to apologize to your family and to you." Edward took two steps closer to the bed. "I should have come sooner, long before this. And said I was sorry a long time ago."

"For what?" Miranda looked genuinely perplexed. "I mean, me and the other servers are the ones that had that party afterwards. Your instructions were very clear and I…well, I didn't listen. If I had, I wouldn't have been in the building that night."

Livia had expected anger from Miranda. After all, the girl had suffered, and she was more than entitled to her share of fury. Instead, she saw a girl who hadn't let the fire beat down her sunny personality. Or let anyone else shoulder the blame for her decisions.

"I should have stayed," Edward said. "It was my hall, and I always make sure everything is right before I leave, but that night…" He threw up his hands. "I have no excuse. I'm sorry this happened to you, Miranda. Deeply sorry."

Her eyes watered. She nodded. "Thank you. And I'm sorry your hall burned down. We never intended for anything to happen."

He crossed to the bed and dropped into the chair across from Miranda. He laid a hand over Miranda's, the same way Livia had done to his earlier. She glanced at his hand and smiled, as if his touch brought her a feeling of acceptance, of forgiveness. "I know, Miranda. I don't blame you at all."

"I thought…" Miranda's lower lip trembled. "I thought you were mad at me for the fire. Like, that's your whole business. And if we hadn't had that party, it wouldn't be gone now."

"I was never mad at you. I stayed away because…" He heaved a sigh. "It was easier than facing what had happened to you. I blame myself entirely."

"Oh, Mr. Graham, don't. I'm going to be okay. I've had to wait before I could start college—" at that a wistfulness filled her eyes, and her gaze swept the album covers on her walls "—but I'll get there soon enough. Maybe not Pratt. I mean, that one's out of my price range, but somewhere."

Edward looked at Livia. Understanding dawned in his eyes. "Well, maybe I can help a bit with that. I have to get something out of the car. I'll be right back."

He hurried out of the room. Piper started to fuss, clearly done with being carried around. Livia shifted the baby's weight to the other hip.

"What's her name?" Miranda asked.

"Piper." Livia saw the interest in the girl's eyes and moved a little closer. "Do you want to meet her?"

Miranda nodded, then hesitated. "But don't you think all this—" she waved a hand over her body "—will scare her?"

"Not at all. Piper might beep your nose—that's her new thing—but she won't be bothered one bit." Livia sat on the edge of the bed, then balanced Piper on her knee. Piper turned toward the new person and made a gaa noise.

Miranda leaned forward, and slid a finger into Piper's fist. "Hey, there, Piper."

Piper gurgled and squeezed Miranda's hand. She kicked her feet and pumped her little fists. Miranda laughed. Wonder filled her face. "I think she likes me."

"What's not to like?" Livia said softly, her voice catching on the last words. "Look at you, Miranda. You're a strong, smart and upbeat girl, despite everything you've been through. A lesser person wouldn't have your attitude, your smile. I can only hope Piper grows up with those same qualities."

Miranda's eyes misted, and she dropped her gaze to the baby. For a long while, she didn't say anything, and neither did Livia. They let Piper do the talking.

Edward came back in the room, holding the bag from the store. He took in the scene on the bed and gave Livia a grateful smile. Then he plopped the bag beside Miranda and returned to his place in the chair. "I think we have just what you need here, so you don't have to put your dreams on hold one more day. Merry Christmas, Miranda."

Edward reached into the bag and pulled out the laptop they had bought earlier. He had questioned Livia about the need for so much memory and a good graphics card, but now she saw that he understood. He added two graphic design software programs to the pile. "Livia and I picked this out earlier today. And we're pretty sure this set up should be just what you need to practice your design work."

For a long second, Miranda didn't say anything. She just stared at the gift, clearly stunned. Then her eyes watered and she hugged the laptop to her chest, the software boxes spilling onto her lap. "Oh my God, this is so awesome. More than I could ever dream of having. Thank you. Thank you so much."

Edward shrugged. "It's nothing. Truly."

Miranda lowered the laptop and cocked her head to study Edward. "But why would you do this for me? I didn't work for you very long, and I burned down your hall and—"

"You didn't destroy anything, Miranda. In fact, this Christmas, I think you helped me make a lot of things very, very right. And if anyone knows the importance of pursuing your dreams, it's me. I started with that banquet hall when I was fresh out of college and it grew into a national business, bigger than I could have imagined. You have a talent. And you need to pursue it."

Miranda sighed. "That's a dream, Mr. Graham. It's way too expensive to go to Pratt and besides, I have to stay here and have surgeries and stuff." She let out another long breath. "Someday, maybe."

"I'm sure you can start online with them."

"Maybe."

He leaned back and feigned thinking. "You know, I'm starting a scholarship fund. It was a scholarship that helped pay for me to go to business college, and without it, I doubt I'd be where I am today. But mine would be more for kids who had suffered…setbacks and needed a little help to get to college."

"That sounds like a great idea."

"And I want you to be the first recipient."

It took a moment for the words to sink in. "Really?" Her eyes widened and a tentative smile appeared on her face.

"Yeah."

"Because of—" she glanced down at the pressure suit and the scars "—what the fire did to me?"

"No. Because of what the fire has taught me." He reached out and laid a gentle hand on her arm. "I can't change the past, but I can change the future. For me, for you, and for other students down the road."

"I'm really going to be able to do this? Really?"

Edward laughed, and for the first time since she'd returned to Riverbend, Livia saw real joy in his features. "Really, really."

"Oh my gosh. Oh my gosh. Oh my gosh!" Miranda's fingers danced along her lips. Then the realization that this was real, and was going to happen, burst on her face like a sunrise. "Dad! Mom! Come here!"

A thunder of footsteps sounded on the stairs. The door burst the rest of the way open and the Willetts hurried in, breathless. Richard cast a sharp glance at Edward. "What'd you do?"

Edward waved toward Miranda. "Let her tell you."

"What is it? Are you okay, honey?" Alicia asked. "Are you in pain?"

"No, I'm fantastic. And I'm going to college. Starting today." She beamed at Edward. "Mr. Graham is giving me a scholarship. I want to check out and see if Pratt is offering online classes, so I can take those until I'm ready for real classes." Then she held up the computer.

"And he bought me this laptop, and all the software I need to design."

"Really?" Her mother stared at Edward, then Miranda.

Miranda laughed. "That's what I said. And he said really, really."

A flush filled Edward's face. "I'm just trying to help us all have a new start here."

Richard shook his head, then put out his hand to shake Edward's. "Seems I've judged you wrong."

"No, you haven't."

"You've done a good thing. More than anyone could ask." Richard swallowed hard then faced Edward. "Thank you."

"No, thank you. You've raised a wonderful and gracious girl. And I hope when she completes that degree, she comes to work for my company."

"You mean it?" Miranda asked.

"Of course. Not as part of the wait staff, but in the offices, helping the marketing department. Unless some record label grabs you first for their marketing arm. We do a lot of concerts at our other venues, Miranda. And I bet you'd be great working in that department."

"I'd love that." She flipped open the laptop and powered it on. "I'm going to get started right now. From this day forward," Miranda said, "my life is changing and I am pursuing my dreams."

"Me too," Edward said softly, as he and Livia and Piper left the room, and the happy, crying Willett family. "Me too."

CHAPTER TEN

"You're gonna wear a hole in that carpet," Ray said from his post by the Christmas tree, where he was hanging a few more ornaments unearthed from the attic that morning. "You're as nervous as a cat in a rocking chair factory."

Edward laughed and stopped his constant motion in front of the window. "Sorry, Dad. I hate waiting."

"Especially when you're waiting on a pretty woman." Ray put the empty box to the side. "A woman who's got your heart?"

Edward stared out the window. The gray day had seemed to brighten, and he could almost smell the coming snow in the air. Or maybe it was just his attitude that had changed. For the first time in forever, he was looking forward to Christmas nearly as much as he had when he'd been a little boy. "I think so."

After the afternoon they'd spent visiting Miranda, Livia had dropped Edward off at his father's house and promised to return for dinner. They hadn't talked much on the ride home—it was close to Piper's nap time and she hadn't been happy about being in the car instead of in her crib at home. So any conversation they tried to have had been interrupted by one very loudly complaining baby. Edward had tried to soothe Piper, since he was in the passenger's seat and more free to reach back there, but she was overtired and having none of it. That little taste of Livia's life made him sympathize with the work she obviously put in raising their child. It wasn't all smiles and beep-beeps on the nose. Yet, even as he'd tried—and failed—to coax a smile to his daughter's face, he'd realized he was doing something far more important.

Being a parent.

It was a new feeling, one he was still trying on, like a new pair of shoes.

When he got home, Edward had gone outside and hit the wood pile again. He'd needed clear, cold air in his lungs and some time to himself. To think. His father had let him chop for an hour, as if sensing his son needed to be alone.

With every swoop of the axe, the world became a little clearer to Edward. It was as if he'd made the first steps today at the Willett house—no, he'd made those first steps when Livia had taken his hand in the nursery and told him it was time to make amends. All afternoon, he'd thought she meant with the Willetts.

The wood stacked up beside him, the scent of freshly slivered logs filling the air. And the healing process began.

Because Edward realized the one he needed to make amends with wasn't Miranda. Or her parents.

But himself.

He had begun, ever so slowly, to open his heart. To his father, to Livia, to Piper, to other people. And it wasn't nearly as difficult as he'd expected.

Now he couldn't wait to see Livia and tell her. Still, he paced, worried that it was too late. That he had damaged their relationship beyond repair.

"Glad to hear you're moving forward. It's about time."
Ray flicked off the television and turned on the stereo.
Classical versions of Christmas music filled the house.
"There. That should set the mood."

Edward chuckled and shook his head. "Since when
did you become Cupid?"

"Since I realized what a good thing a great wife can
be." Ray's eyes brimmed with emotion, but he shrugged
it off with a gruff gust. "You better realize that, too, my
boy. You're not getting any younger."

"Nothing's stopping you from dating again yourself,
you know."

Ray patted his chest. "Once this ticker's ready to rock,
I'll be taking some twirls on the dance floor again."

"Good for you."

"I'm glad you did what you did today for the Willett
girl," Ray said. "Just talking to her and the family was
a big step. One in the right direction."

"Yeah." Edward let out a long breath. It hadn't been
easy, and had been a moment he'd resisted for a year,
but the look on Miranda's face had made it all worth-
while. "I agree."

"So…you still going to sell the company?"

Edward thought about it for a moment. He had an
offer on the table for his company—a generous one and
one that could let him sit around and count his money
for years. He'd already achieved his financial goals—to
become a millionaire before he was thirty—but found
once he had the money in his account, that there was no
better or greater challenge than the next one. It wasn't
about the money. It was about seeing if he could grow
the company to new levels every year. Expand beyond
banquet halls and into concert venues, then to theaters
and outdoor amphitheaters. To go nationwide, then

maybe someday, global. In the end, though, it was that very challenge that had been part of what cost him his relationship with Livia.

Could he still do that, but manage to be here and be involved? He thought of Livia, then Piper. That alone was enough motivation to find a way to have it all. "I'm going to keep the company, but I'm going to do things differently from here on out."

"How?"

"I'm going to make time. So that in the end—" he glanced out the window and watched as Livia pulled into the driveway, with their daughter tucked safely in the back seat, making his heart leap and his pulse race "—I don't have a single regret."

Ray clapped his son on the shoulder. "I'm proud of you, son." His voice was hoarse, and he let out a little cough, covering for the emotion, then he turned away and settled into his recliner.

The doorbell rang and Edward crossed to answer it. He pulled open the door to see Livia and Piper, their cheeks rosy from the cold. Behind them was Melody, holding a foil-covered dish. Edward's heart sang, and he had to force himself not to crush Livia in a hug.

"Merry Christmas," Edward said, the words feeling a little foreign on his tongue. Geez, had it been that long since he'd felt festive? "Well, Christmas Eve."

She smiled one of the hundred different smiles of hers that he loved. "Merry Christmas to you, too."

"We brought mac and cheese," Melody said, holding up the dish. The sharp scent of cheddar cheese wafted up to greet him. "Livia disagrees, but in my opinion, carbs go with everything. And mac and cheese...well, that's the bomb."

"It's whole wheat pasta," Livia added. "Only slightly unhealthy."

Edward chuckled. Leave it to Livia to health up an artery-clogging dish. "Thank you. I know my dad's going to be in heaven." He slid the diaper bag off Livia's arm and put it on his own. "Come on in."

"I'm going to go put this in the oven to warm up," Melody said. "Three-fifty, right?"

Livia nodded, and Melody headed off to the kitchen. Livia waved a greeting at Edward's father. "Nice to see you again, Mr. Graham."

"Oh, you know it's always Ray to you, Miss Livia." He gestured toward his son, and didn't move out of his recliner. Maybe his father was feeling bad today, which sent a rush of concern through Edward. "Hey, Edward, go get my grandbaby for me, and bring her to me. Let Livia have a minute to herself without her arms all full."

Edward reached out, and Piper leaned toward him, her face animated and happy. She settled into his arms without complaint and laid her head on his shoulder. Her weight felt comfortable against him, almost…perfect. His fingers brushed against the soft dewy skin of her legs where her jumper had ridden up, and he inhaled the strawberry sweet scent of her skin. She was…perfect. Absolutely freaking perfect.

A curious feeling of peace and joy stole over Edward and settled in the deepest recesses of his heart. So this was what it felt like.

Damn.

And he'd almost missed it. Almost given it all up. Almost.

"I think she recognizes her father," Livia said softly. She rested her hand on Piper's back and smiled at the scene before her.

"I think you're right." He reached up and hesitated only a second before placing a palm against the downy hair on the back of Piper's head. She curved into the touch and cooed. In that instant, he felt a swell of something that he was pretty sure was love.

She was his daughter. And she knew it.

He leaned in and met Piper's face with his own. She stared at him, blinking. Then her lips widened, and he could swear a smile curved across her face. "Hey there."

Piper gurgled and bounced in his arms. She reached out and grabbed his nose. Livia stood to the side, watching them. She looked ready to grab the baby at any time, but Edward had this under control. And he wanted to prove that to Livia. Prove he was ready—and willing—to step into his role as Piper's father.

He reached out and pressed a finger to Piper's nose. "Beep."

She laughed, and bounced some more. Squeezed his nose so hard, he was surprised she didn't break it.

So he did it again. "Beep!"

She squealed and bounced again and again. Her eyes were wide—his eyes, the same blue—and her face was lit with joy. An echoing feeling exploded inside him. So this was what it was like. Amazing.

So he did it again. "Beep!"

They played the game over and over again, and each time, Piper got more and more excited. Finally, Edward stopped—to protect his own nose, which was beginning to hurt. He crossed to his father and settled Piper in Ray's lap. "Careful. The kid's got quite the grip."

When he looked at Piper, Ray's entire demeanor melted like ice cream under the sun. "Hey, kiddo."

She stared at him, unblinking. Then Piper turned to look at Edward, and her face broke into a smile.

Ray glanced up at Edward. He grinned. "Seems she knows who her daddy is."

"She does indeed." Edward ruffled Piper's hair. Then he realized that his father wasn't feeling bad at all—he'd merely been concocting a way to get his son to handle Piper. "You're a smart man, Dad."

Ray chuckled. "You gotta be to raise a son like you." Then Ray reached out and trailed a finger along Piper's cheek. "Ah, kiddo…you look just like another Piper I know."

Edward's heart nearly broke for his father. He could hear the pain in Ray's voice, but it was mixed with wonder and happiness, too. As if this little fifteen pounds of baby had finally healed a wound that had been open far too long. Edward could feel it in the room, and when his gaze connected with Livia's he saw that she did, too. He bent down beside his father, and let Piper's fingers curl around his thumb. "She does, doesn't she?"

They both could see it—the features that so resembled Katie's. It was as if God had given the Graham family a second chance to make it right. To open their circle this time, rather than closing it off like before. Edward watched Ray marvel over his granddaughter and decided that nothing was going to keep him from being a part of Piper's life.

A beeping sounded in the kitchen and Melody came rushing into the room. "Uh, something's going off. I hope I didn't burn the casserole."

"It's probably the ham. I can get it." Ray started to rise.

"Don't worry about it, Ray. I can take care of it," Livia said and followed Melody into the kitchen.

"Go." Ray shooed at Edward. "Finish dinner for me,

if you don't mind. I'm going to spend some time with my granddaughter."

"Don't let her wear you out. You're supposed to be resting."

"I will, I promise." Ray sighed, then smiled. "I guess I'll follow my doctor's orders a little closer. I want to be around to teach this sweet little girl how to reel in a bass."

Edward smiled and gave his father's shoulder a squeeze. "I'm glad to hear that, Dad. Really glad."

Ray's hand covered Edward's. "Me, too." The two men's eyes met and then they each looked away. They were still Grahams, after all, and a mushy moment wasn't part of the family DNA.

Livia couldn't stay busy enough in the kitchen. She removed the ham from the oven, then turned off the timer, and set to work carving it. She knew she should let the meat rest, but she didn't want to go back in the living room and face Edward. Not yet.

What did he want? Every time he turned around, he told her he didn't want to be a father, didn't want to be anything more than a financial donor in Piper's life, that he was the same man he had been before, closed off emotionally. And then just now, he played with her, engaged with her—

And got her hopes up.

"Damn!" Livia put down the knife.

Melody arched a brow. "What did that ham ever do to you? That thing's a mess. Here, let me do it."

"You? Carve a ham?" Livia let out a snort. "Right."

"I'm not totally incompetent in the kitchen," Melody said, then she grinned. "I just act that way so you'll wait on me."

Livia swatted her sister, then stepped away from the carving board. Melody had a point—Livia did cater to her sister. Perhaps if she stepped away more often, Melody wouldn't be so dependent. She made a vow to let Melody stand on her own two feet from here on out. "I don't know what's wrong with me."

"You're all discombobulated by a man. I know. I've been there myself." Melody sliced the ham into perfectly even pieces, and used the knife to lay them in a concentric pattern on the platter. Exactly the way Livia had done it a hundred times. Apparently Melody had been paying attention.

"I am not," Livia hissed. She turned toward the cabinet and started reaching for plates so Melody wouldn't see the lie in her eyes. She was discombobulated by Edward, but she was in no mood to talk about it. All she could hope was for dinner to go quickly. Thank goodness Melody had been feeling better and well enough to come along, and hopefully run a little interference.

Ever since they'd left the Willett house, Livia had been torn—between wanting to believe in the Edward she had seen today and being afraid that it wouldn't last. That just when she began to depend on him, to be there, to be a part of her life, he'd shut down and close her out.

"Mmm-hmm," Melody said, clearly not believing her sister at all. Then her voice brightened. "Oh, hi, Edward. Come to help?"

Livia stilled, her hand on the pile of dinner plates. Just hearing his name made her heart trip. Maybe she should have never settled in Riverbend if it was always going to remind her of that man. Best choice for Piper or not, running into him all the time—or hearing people talk about him—was going to be painful.

"Let me get those." His voice was dark and low over her shoulder, and she wanted to melt into his chest.

She didn't.

"Sure." She spun away and nearly winged her hip when she yanked open the silverware drawer. The forks and knives shuddered with a metal clatter.

"I'm going to go put this on the table," Melody said and then disappeared with the platter of ham, leaving Edward and Livia alone.

"I should get the table set," Livia said, grabbing a bunch of silverware and turning away from the drawer. At the same time, Edward turned toward her. The tines of the forks and blades of the butter knives came within inches of his stomach.

He smiled. "You're a dangerous woman."

"Sorry. I'll—" She ducked to the right, but he put a hand on her arm.

"Why are you avoiding me?"

"I'm not. I'm…busy."

He took the silverware out of her hands and laid it on the counter. "Now you're not."

"We have to get the table set for dinner. The ham will get cold—"

"Ham tastes just as good cold as it does warm. It can wait. I want to talk to you." He tipped a finger under her chin and turned her face until she was looking at him. "Why are you avoiding me?"

She wanted to leave the room, but Edward blocked her way. He wanted an answer, and she owed him at least that. Maybe then he would drop it and see that they weren't made for each other. That what she wanted and what he was willing to give were totally different things.

"I…I saw what you did for Miranda," she said. "You

did even more than I thought you would. In that moment, you were an Edward I never saw before."

"And why is that a bad thing?"

"Because…" She couldn't say it. Couldn't look at him. She turned away, unable to voice the words that had tumbled inside her all afternoon.

Because I fell in love with you again when I saw that.

"Because." A lame answer, but the only one she was going to give him.

Edward studied her for a long second, then he turned to call over his shoulder. "Dad, Livia and I are going to take a walk. You and Melody should eat. You don't have to wait on us."

"If that ham's ready, I'm not waiting on anything," his father shouted back from the living room.

"Take care of the baby, will you?"

Ray chuckled. "You know I will. In fact, I'm going to spoil her mercilessly and shower her with noisy toys."

Edward chuckled, then tugged two winter coats off the hook by the back door and held one out to Livia. "Come on. I want to talk to you."

"Edward—"

"Just hear me out. If you don't like what I have to say, you can always come back for ham and macaroni." He held the coat and waited for her to take it.

She shrugged one arm into the jacket, then hesitated. "Piper—"

"Will be fine. Your sister is here and so is my dad. Who happens to have a little childcare experience of his own." Edward slid Livia's other arm into the coat. "I turned out reasonably well, so I'm sure Piper will do just fine."

She'd run out of excuses. So she buttoned her coat, waited for him to do the same, and then they headed out into the cold together. The temperature had dropped a few degrees while they were inside, and Livia closed the neck of the coat against the slight wind. They walked down the driveway and turned right onto the sidewalk. Some of the holiday lights were coming on, as dusk deepened its hues from pale pink to dark purple.

"First, I want to thank you." Edward's words frosted in the cold. "For the shopping trip and for getting me to see Miranda and her family today. How did you know that's what I needed?"

She sidestepped a crack in the sidewalk. "I know you pretty well."

"That you do. Better than I know myself." He slid a glance her way. "You're quite the mind reader. I had no idea how much I needed to do that—not just for Miranda, but for myself—until after we left."

"You're welcome," Livia said. Now Miranda and Edward could move forward. There was that, at least, to take comfort in. "She seemed really happy with the laptop."

"All thanks to you." He chuckled. "I didn't know what you were thinking when you had me buy it. But I trusted you. Good thing."

She shrugged. "I just tried to think like you today at the store. I knew if you got past the fear of seeing her, that you'd want to do something for her. And you had mentioned her wanting to go to college for graphic design, so that seemed like the perfect gift."

He chuckled. "You thought like me? How'd that work out?"

"Well for a while there, I was tempted to watch a football game and have a few beers."

He laughed. "Glad you didn't."

"It is Christmas Eve, after all. I'll save that for the

Super Bowl." She flashed him a grin, then sobered. "I thought the scholarship was a very generous idea."

"What good is money if I can't give to other people? I've made more than enough, and I don't need much to live on. All this time, that money has pretty much sat in the bank, not doing a damned bit of good. Though I have tried to take care of my dad. He lives in the same house we've always lived in, still stokes his woodstove with wood he chops himself, even though I've offered to build him a brand-new house, pay his heating bills for the rest of his life, whatever he wants. He does it because he says there's history in that house. Roots. The things he believes in and holds dear. And no amount of money can give him that."

Livia smiled. She hadn't realized that Edward's cantankerous father had such sentimental tendencies. "Who knew an old softie lurked under Ray's gruff exterior?"

"He just does that to keep up appearances." Edward paused while they turned the corner onto Maple Street. "He's not the only one."

"You're not like your father."

"I'm more like my father than I ever realized." He shoved his hands into the pockets of his coat. "My father worked a million hours a week when I was a kid. He was never home, and it got worse after Katie died. He never talked, never told me how he was feeling. We had almost no relationship. He was doing exactly what I've always done—running away from the pain instead of dealing with it."

"He suffered a terrible loss. It's to be expected, I'm sure." If she ever lost Piper, she had no idea how she'd ever go on again. A loss like that was too big to comprehend, to even begin to wrap her mind around. She could only imagine how hard it had been for the Grahams.

"Yes, but he did all that at the cost of the child he already had. I never saw my father. I didn't get to know him until after my mother died. And even then, our relationship was strained at best, until he had his heart attack. We're still learning how to build a relationship together. I did the same thing with you after the fire. I kept telling myself it would be better if I worked through how I felt alone. That's how I always operated—feelings tucked inside, as if that helped anything. It didn't. All I did was drive a wedge between us." Edward stopped walking and faced Livia. "I don't want that to happen with me and Piper."

"It won't. I'll be sure you see her as much as you want to."

"I want to see her every day."

Livia nodded. He was going to be a part of their daughter's life. It was what she had hoped for, all this time. Then why did she hesitate? "Okay. I'm sure we can work something out."

"No, you're not understanding me, Livia. I want to put Piper to bed and I want to wake up in the morning and see her. I want to watch her smear oatmeal on her face and hear her laugh when I blow bubbles into the air. I want to teach her to ride a bike and warn her about teenage boys, and see her go off to school in the morning." Edward reached for Livia's hands and held them in his own. His deep blue gazed locked on hers. "I want us to be a family, Livia. A real family." He took a deep breath, then smiled. "I want to marry you."

Marry Edward.

It was what she'd wanted him to say—what she'd prayed to hear from the day she found out she was pregnant. She had what she'd told him she wanted now, but as the words sank in and the cold air settled around her, she hesitated again. A choking fear rose in her chest. She pulled her hands out of his and stepped back. "I...I can't do that, Edward. We didn't date very long and just because we have a baby is no reason to get married and..." her voice trailed off. The rush of excuses exhausted.

"And you're terrified to settle down." He closed the distance between them, and his deep blue gaze met hers. Knowing, understanding and seeing past her walls. "For all your talk, Olivia Perkins, deep down inside you're afraid to make a permanent connection."

"I am not."

"Oh yeah? Prove it to me." He tipped her chin to meet his. "Marry me."

Her heart raced so fast, she was sure it would beat right out of her chest. She caught a deep breath, held it. This was what she wanted. Why didn't she just say yes? "I need some time to think about this."

He let out a gust. "You know, all this time I thought it was just me who had the problem opening up, making a commitment. But I'm getting the feeling that either you don't really want me or you don't want to be tied down."

"I..." She exhaled, then faced the truth. It had been there, all this time, heck, all her life, and she'd never had to say it aloud. Until now. "I don't want to be let down."

His gaze softened. "Like your mother did to you and Melody."

She nodded and cursed the tears that rose in her eyes. She thought of the future Edward was proposing and felt nothing but fear. So many things could go wrong. They could start with the best of intentions, and end up apart. The one hurt the most by that would be Piper. Her protective instincts warned her to step away, to head off the damage before it started. "What's to stop you from leaving next week or next month or next year? Raising a child is hard, Edward. It's demanding. Babies are crying and dirty and needy—all the time. And you're going to have days when you are going to want to run away and let someone else do the tough work."

"I'm sure we'll both have those days. But we can get through it together. Give us a chance, Livia."

She turned away and fingered a swag of white lights draped across a short picket fence bordering the sidewalk. The sun had dropped behind the horizon and all around her, Christmas lights began to come on, blinking their little bits of magic. "After my mother left," she said, "I vowed that when I grew up, my kids would have a perfect Christmas. Trees and stockings and wreaths and everything they needed. And I tried this year, I really did. I wanted Piper to have everything I never had. And—" her voice broke "—I still failed."

"You didn't fail at all. You're a wonderful mother. That's the only gift she needs."

"No, that's not true. I didn't get her the one gift she really wants."

"What's that?"

She shook her head and pulled away. He hadn't said the words and she wasn't going to force them out of him. Love, she wanted to scream, that was what she was looking for. He had opened up so much already, but he had yet to open his heart all the way to her. Without that, she couldn't take a chance. "I can't do this, Edward."

"You mean you can't take a risk."

"What if it doesn't work out? What will happen to Piper then?" She glanced out at the neighborhood, all looking so peaceful and perfect.

"Aren't you the one who lectured me about not worrying about the things you can't control?"

"But don't you see? I can control this. I can head this off before it disintegrates. Before Piper is left—" Livia cut off her sentence. And now the tears came anyway, strong and determined. "To raise herself."

"Oh, Livia," he said, softly, reaching for her, "that wouldn't happen."

She stepped away from him, putting as much distance between them as she could on the small sidewalk. She turned her face up to the dark, clear sky. "I wish it would snow. Then Piper's first Christmas would be perfect."

"It still can be." He took her hand, ran his fingers along hers. "Believe in miracles, Livia. They can and do happen."

She shook her head. How many times had she tried to believe in the miracle of her mother's return? Of things that never happened, never came to pass? No, it was far better that she protect Piper now, rather than leave her daughter in the same situation later in life. "I believe in what I can see, Edward. And I don't see a future for us. I thought l did, but I was wrong."

Then she headed back to his father's house to collect her child and to leave before she put stock in something that could never be.

CHAPTER ELEVEN

EDWARD stood by the Christmas tree in his father's front room, watching the multicolored lights blink on and off. The scent of ham and macaroni and cheese still lingered in the air, but the holiday spirit had left when Livia did. His father was in the kitchen, cursing over a crossword puzzle.

How had that gone so wrong? He'd been sure, when he asked her to marry him that she'd say yes. He wanted the same thing she did—a family. He loved her, he wanted to be with her and Piper…what could be holding her back?

The doorbell rang, dragging Edward out of his thoughts. "Earl," he said when he answered the door. "What brings you by on Christmas Eve?"

Earl doffed his plaid hunting cap and gave Edward a hearty hello. "I wanted to thank you for working the tree lot."

"No problem. It was my pleasure."

Earl handed him two slim pieces of paper. "It ain't much, in the way of thank-yous, but I figured you'd get some enjoyment out of these. My Betsy and I are going, so we're hoping to see you all there, too."

"Two tickets to the New Year's Eve party at Rustica?"

Edward started to hand them back, then reconsidered. He gave Earl a grin. "You do know you are the most obvious matchmaker in Riverbend, don't you?"

Earl chuckled. "All I'm trying to do is build up Riverbend's population. It's my civic duty."

"I don't think Cupid ever thought of that angle."

Earl tapped his head. "Some of us are smarter than your average guy in diapers."

Edward laughed. "Well, that population is definitely increasing by one. I'm moving back. And rebuilding the hall. In fact, I'm moving my corporate headquarters here, too, so I'll be around a lot more."

"That's really good to hear." Earl clapped Edward on the shoulder. "So…is there any hope you'll be living in a house built for three?"

"I don't know about that." He sighed and crossed his arms over his chest. "I asked her to marry me. She turned me down."

"Hell, I've asked Betsy three times." Earl grinned. "She's a stubborn woman, my Betsy."

"What are you going to do?"

He shrugged. "Keep asking. A man can't give up on the woman he loves. I know Betsy. She'll come around." He planted his cap on his head and redid the flaps. "She's a worrywart, and I think she just wants to know that I love her more than anything under the sun, and that I'll always be around, before she puts my ring on her finger."

"Earl, you're a fixture in this place. I can't imagine you going anywhere."

"That's what I keep telling Betsy. That she's stuck with me till the end of time." Earl turned and took a step off the porch, then turned back. "Looks like snow."

"That's what they keep saying. But it hasn't happened yet."

"Just keep believing," Earl said. "You never know what Santa will bring you on Christmas mornin'."

Melody had been following Livia around for the better part of an hour. She'd stuck close to her when she put Piper down for a nap. Hovered while Livia started a load of laundry and folded another one. And always with the same goal—to try to get Livia to talk about Edward. Which Livia had thus far avoided doing, ever since they left Ray's house. But Melody was not easily deterred.

"I brought home some leftovers for you," Melody said. "It's not good to go around on an empty stomach."

Livia threw the last few pieces of dirty laundry into the machine and added some detergent. "Hey, that's my advice."

"Yup. I listen more than you think, too."

"Well…good." Livia pushed start on the washer, then leaned against the machine. "I'm sorry. Thank you for helping at Ray's and for packing up some leftovers for me. I appreciate it."

"Enough to tell me what happened on that walk?"

"I really don't want to talk about that." She tried to leave the laundry room, but Melody blocked her exit.

"I know you think I'm bad at relationships."

"I never said that."

"You didn't have to. It's practically public knowledge." Melody let out a little self-deprecating laugh. "But at least I know why I run instead of stay. Carl's screw-up notwithstanding, most of the time, it's me leaving, even when things are great. Like you just did."

"I don't—"

"You do. You ran from Riverbend when things didn't work out between you and Edward. And once he was gone, you ran right back here. Because it was safe to— he'd already left. No danger of running into him again."

"Or so I thought."

"And you know why you do that?"

Livia propped a fist on her hip. "Hey, when did you become the analyst of my love life?"

"Since forever. You're my big sister, Liv. I watched everything you did." A tender smile stole across Melody's face, a rare moment of vulnerability in a sister who didn't like to let others peek inside her soul. "And I tried to live up to the example you set."

"You did?" Livia had never realized that about Melody. She'd been so busy worrying about making sure Melody was brought up right, that she never lacked for love or attention, that she hadn't thought about an example.

"Of course I did," Melody said. "I loved you and envied you and copied you all my life. You're my big sister."

Sister. Not surrogate mother, but sister. The kind of sister you played checkers with and joked with, and shared memories with. *Sister.*

"You really think of me as your sister?" Livia asked. A smile curved across her face, and she felt her shoulders ease, as if the burden she had put on herself when she'd stepped into the maternal role all those years ago had finally eased.

Melody nodded. "Yup, sisters. Complete with all the fights over boys and hair products, and sweater sharing." There was a tease in her voice, but no mistaking the love there, too.

Livia drew Melody into a warm, tight hug. She held her little sister for a long time, while tears dampened each of their shoulders. "I love you, Mel."

"I love you too, Livia." Then Melody drew back and cupped Livia's face. Melody's green eyes were serious, and determined. "This time, I'm going to tell *you* what to do. Because I think you've been worrying too much about everyone else—me, Piper, heck, the people in this town—than you have about finding your own happiness."

"I don't…" Then Livia considered her sister's words. How many years had she done exactly that? Shelving her own life, to take care of those around her. It had become second nature, and even now, when she knew in her heart that she loved Edward, she kept pushing him away. "Maybe I do."

Melody nodded, and a knowing look lit her eyes. "So, take the smelly monkey to the Winterfest. Let her see Santa. And then go track down that hunk of a guy who's madly in love with you and tell him you want to marry him."

"How do you know he's madly in love with me?"

"It's written all over his face, sis. He was so starry-eyed, he was practically tripping over his feet today." Melody let out a long sigh. "I would give my right arm to have a man look at me like that."

"You will someday."

Melody waved that off. "We'll worry about someday later. Right now, you have an amazing man to go find. So go." She took Livia's arm and practically dragged her out of the laundry room. "You can even borrow my sweater if you want."

Just before she left, Livia turned to her sister and gave

her one more hug. "You're the smartest and best sister anyone could ask for."

"That's 'cause I learned from the best," Melody said with a smile.

The Winterfest party was in full swing by the time Edward arrived. He had a few hours until the clock turned past midnight, and Christmas Eve gave way to Christmas Day. Some time yet to pull off a miracle.

At first, he didn't see Livia anywhere. Had her sister been wrong when he'd stopped by the house, looking for Livia? Had Livia opted out of the Winterfest after all?

Then he saw her, Piper perched on one hip, standing before the gingerbread family display. Piper was reaching for the brightly lit people, clearly fascinated. Edward hung back for a moment, just watching his daughter take in the world. Everything was a discovery for her—new people, new situations, new experiences. And if everything worked out, he'd be right there, catching every single second.

Livia turned just then—did she sense him behind her?—and a smile curved across her heart-shaped face. It was yet another of the dozens of smiles of hers that he loved. Then the smile disappeared, and as he closed the distance between them, he started praying for a miracle again.

"What are you doing here?" she said.

"Looking for you. And my daughter." He took a step forward, and as he did, Piper noticed him and leaned toward him. He grinned like a fool, ridiculously happy every time his child recognized him. Such a simple thing, and yet so huge to him. "It's Christmas. We should spend it together."

"You want to go to the Winterfest. With us."

It wasn't even a question. It was more disbelief framed in a sentence. "Why is that so hard to believe?"

"Because you're not a holiday guy."

"Hey, don't judge me by that tree. My dad and I aren't exactly decorators." He took another step forward, noting Piper still leaning in his direction. Then the joke faded from his voice, and he caught Livia's gaze with his own. "You're right. Up until this year, I wasn't much of a holiday guy. I guess after Katie died, Christmas was never the same. I never really felt like celebrating again."

"I know what you mean. We tried, after my mother left, but it was like there was always a hole." She sighed and fiddled with Piper's snowsuit.

"Exactly. I thought I was just fine like that, fine being by myself, but I was wrong." He waited until her gaze met his. "When you left the house tonight, that's what I felt. Like there was a hole where my family should be. I don't want to feel that way anymore, Livia."

"Edward…I can't." She spun away, and Piper let out a squeal of protest. She leaned her little body over Livia's shoulder, making her intentions clear. Piper wanted her daddy, but her mother was speeding off in the opposite direction.

Then the answer came to him, so fast and furious, it was like a slap upside the head. Livia wanted proof. Tangible proof that he was serious. That he loved her and their daughter, and he wasn't going to run from any of that. That was the one thing he had never given her before. She'd fallen for him last year, and he'd kept all his emotional cards close to his chest. Time to let them show.

He stepped around Livia, stopping her departure, and put his hands out. Piper bounced and reached again. "Can I hold her?"

Livia hesitated only a fraction of an instant. Then she read the body language of her daughter, and the clear interest of her daughter's father, and handed Piper to him. The baby settled against Edward's chest and began to coo. Wonder filled Livia's features. "Look at her. She's so…happy."

"Good." He nuzzled a kiss along Piper's forehead. The action felt so natural, so right, he couldn't believe he hadn't done it before. He vowed to do all of this a lot more often. "Now, what say we get your mommy to come with us for a little while?"

Livia shook her head. "I should probably be getting her to bed. It's getting late."

"Piper, tell your mommy that she's never going to believe I can be a great dad and a great husband if she doesn't give me a chance to prove it to her." He nuzzled Piper again, and she let out a stream of baby babble.

"Edward—"

"Don't forget to tell Mommy that Christmas is no time for arguing." Edward took Piper's hand and helped the baby wag a cautioning finger at Livia. "See? She agrees."

Livia opened her mouth again, as if she might do that very thing, then shut it again. She rolled her eyes, but a grin played at the corners of her lips. "You win. Or rather, Piper does. Where are we going?"

"To tell Santa what we want for Christmas. If you don't tell him, he can't bring it." Edward beeped Piper's nose, which made the baby squeal with delight. "Isn't that right, Piper?"

"Okay, but just for a little while. It is, after all, almost bedtime." Livia walked alongside Edward as they crossed the park, waving to people they knew, and headed for the small red house marked Santa's Village.

C.J. Hamilton sat in the big chair on the porch of the little house, decked out as the big guy himself, looking pretty realistic in his thick white beard and bushy eyebrows, too. Clearly, he'd brought a lot of Hollywood tricks with him when he'd moved to Riverbend. Beside him stood his wife, Jessica, in a matching red dress and black boots, a perfect Mrs. Claus. In a pen to the right of Santa's house was a live reindeer—an annual fixture at the Winterfest and a kid favorite. Tonight, though, the line of children was down to just one, probably because most of them wanted to get home early in case Santa dropped down their chimney first. When the last child left, C.J. reached for Piper.

"Ho, ho, ho. Who do we have here?" C.J. did a perfect imitation of Kris Kringle, complete with a shake of his temporary pillow-formed jelly belly.

"Piper Graham," Edward said, leaning forward to place his daughter on C.J.'s lap.

C.J. glanced up at Edward with a blink of surprise. "Seems Santa has already blessed your house this year."

"He has." Edward felt a goofy grin spread across his face. Proud as hell to show off his beautiful daughter. Why had he ever thought he didn't want this? Right now, he wanted to shout it from the rooftops, tell it to the world, that this incredible child was his. "He has indeed."

"Congratulations," Jessica said, drawing Livia into a quick hug. "She's beautiful."

"Thank you." Livia watched her daughter, sitting on Santa's lap and delighting at the new face. And Edward watched them both, completely smitten with the girls in his life.

"Well, well, little girl, what do you want for Christmas?" C.J. leaned in toward Piper, as if she might whisper in his ear. Instead she grabbed his beard and gave it a tug. "Ah, she says she wants a beard of her own."

Edward and Livia laughed. "If she ends up with a beard," Livia said. "I'm going to have a long talk with my obstetrician."

"I'm thinking…teddy bear," C.J. said, gently untangling his beard from Piper's grasp. "What do you say, Piper?"

She babbled and bounced. Apparently in complete agreement. C.J. laughed, gave Piper a little tap on the nose, then handed her back to Edward. He and Livia said goodbye to C.J. and Jessica and started across the park again. All around them, people were soaking up the last few hours of the Winterfest—playing at the carnival games, sipping at hot chocolate, nibbling at pretzels.

"I can take her if she's getting too heavy," Livia said.

"She's just fine. Isn't that right?" Edward glanced over at Piper, and she gave him a toothless grin. "I think we're about all done at the Winterfest. But before you run back home, Livia, I want to show you something."

"What?"

"You'll have to trust me just a little longer to find out." With Piper balanced on one hip, he took Livia's hand, and together they headed out of the park and across the street. He glanced up at the sky and hoped Mother Nature would cooperate with his plan. If not, he'd improvise.

"The tree lot?" Livia paused when they stopped at their destination, her brows knitted in confusion. "Isn't it closed now?"

"Yup. But there was one tree left. One lonely little tree, with no one to love it." He tugged her around the corner, to a small stubby tree, too short for most people's tastes, and too tall for a tabletop. He'd plopped it into a metal tree stand earlier tonight, and done his best to take it from scraggly to Christmasy.

"Did you do this?" She crossed to the tree and fingered the strings of lights decorating the tree, the scattering of red and gold ornaments dangling from the branches. It wasn't much, but it was the best he could do in such a short period of time and with his own admittedly limited decorating skills. From her seat in his arms, Piper stared at the tree, fascinated by the lights. "Why?"

"Because I thought our first tree should be just ours. And, this tree lot was where we started again—"

"I remember. The wreath. And the cup of coffee. And that kiss." Her smile widened, and he hoped it was because she enjoyed the memories. Because he did—especially the kiss.

"I thought it would be special to return here," he said, "with you and my daughter. To start our first Christmas together, right here."

Her gaze roamed over the tree again. "It's…perfect. I love it, Edward. Thank you."

He came up behind her, and his breath whispered along her neck, lifting the delicate tendrils of her dark hair. How he wanted to kiss her, hold her. "Santa forgot to ask you what you want for Christmas, Livia."

"Nothing. I have everything I need." She gave her daughter's hand a little squeeze, then met his gaze. "Really, I do."

"Oh, I don't know about that." He bent down, Piper balanced on his hip, and withdrew a package from beneath the tree. "Let's give this to Mommy, okay?" Piper gurgled and bounced in agreement. He gave her a kiss on the temple and she reached for his nose, keeping up the constant stream of baby babble. "Piper says, 'Open it.'"

Livia took the package from him and gave him a curious look. "What's this?"

"Open it and see."

She undid the wrapping paper. It fluttered to the ground in a big red and green square. He watched her, waiting, his breath caught in his throat, for the moment when it all clicked. Then, there it was, a sharp inhale of breath, and the smile that he had grown to love lit up her face, her eyes, everything. "A cookie jar Santa?"

He nodded.

Tears welled in her eyes, and she clutched the box to her chest. A porcelain Santa face, jolly, merry, ready for holidays to come, decorated the front. "Edward…I…oh, my, it's exactly right. Just the kind I always imagined. That one silly little thing I missed at Christmas."

"It's not silly, not at all. I want every Christmas from here on out to be perfect, for both of us. No more ghosts from the past, Livia. We can start fresh, this year, this moment. The three of us." He tipped his head toward the box. "And the cookie jar Santa."

"I…I don't know what to say."

She'd already said it all, with the look on her face. He'd hoped, when he bought the silly kitschy thing and wrapped it earlier this evening, that she would see the gift the way he did—as a new beginning, where nothing was missing. And then, as if Mother Nature agreed, something white whispered past Livia's cheek, then another, and another.

"Oh my. It's snowing." Livia turned her face to the sky, to meet the first snowflakes. They tumbled fast and thick, coating the branches of the tree with white. "Just in time for Piper's first Christmas."

He smiled. "I told you to believe in miracles."

"You did." She caught a sprinkling of snow in her palm, blew it off, then caught another handful. "That's a hard thing for a control freak to do."

"I know. You're preaching to the choir, Livia." Then he nodded toward the gift, his heart caught in his throat. "There's more. Look inside."

"What? Cookies too?" She opened the box, and pried off the lid of the cookie jar. A gasp escaped her, and she paused before reaching inside to pull out the small velvet box.

Before Livia could say anything, Edward took the box from her and got down on one knee, balancing Piper on the other leg. He held the ring box out to Livia, cupped in both his large palm and Piper's little one. The baby looked down at the soft box, probably wondering if she could eat it.

"I know getting married is a huge leap of faith for you. Faith in me, in us. But hear me out."

She bit her lip and nodded.

"From this day forward, I want us to be a family," he said. "We'll live here, in a little house on a quiet side street, and teach Piper to walk and ride a bike and dig for bugs." Livia smiled at the last, and he took that as a good sign, and kept talking. "I promise to make you happy, to make you smile, because I sure as hell love your smiles, Livia. Every single one of them. But most of all, I promise to be there and to talk to you, and let you in my heart, my soul. Today, tomorrow and all the days after that." Tears glimmered anew in her eyes, and she bit her lip in that way he loved. He thumbed open the box's lid. "Because I love you, Livia, and I love our daughter, and I want you to marry me, and make us a family."

Piper let out a soft coo, as if she was marveling at the ring, too. Edward pressed his head to Piper's and inhaled her sweet, incredible baby scent. While he waited for the answer to the most important question he'd ever asked.

"I…I love you too," Livia said, but still she didn't take the ring. "I always have. I'm just so afraid, Edward."

He rose, put the box in her palm and covered her hand with his own. "Then stand next to me, Livia. I'll hold on to you." He held her gaze, steady and sure. "I'm not going anywhere. Ever."

The tears brimmed on her eyelashes, then slid down in one slow trickle. He could see her struggle with letting go, with trusting. She took in a deep breath, then met his gaze, the cookie jar Santa still clutched to her chest. Her green eyes locked on his and after what seemed an interminable moment, she nodded, and a smile burst on her face. "Yes, Edward, yes, I'll marry you."

His heart exploded with joy. He drew Livia into a tight embrace, creating the warm, perfect circle of him,

Livia and Piper. He'd been all over the world, to every major destination there was, and yet he couldn't imagine another place he would rather be than right here in this little town standing by this sad little tree with the woman and daughter he loved.

She drew back and looked up at him with a smile. Between them, Piper babbled softly. "You never told me what you want for Christmas, Edward."

"I already have it all," Edward said softly, then kissed his wife-to-be as the snow dusted them with a winter kiss. "And I'm never letting it go. Merry Christmas, Livia."

"Merry Christmas, Edward." Then she curved into his arms, and completed his life.

* * * * *

CLASSIC

Quintessential, modern love stories
that are romance at its finest.

COMING NEXT MONTH
AVAILABLE JANUARY 10, 2012

#4285 MASTER OF THE OUTBACK
Margaret Way

#4286 THE RELUCTANT PRINCESS
Raye Morgan

#4287 THE BALLERINA BRIDE
Once Upon a Kiss...
Fiona Harper

#4288 MARDIE AND THE CITY SURGEON
Banksia Bay
Marion Lennox

**#4289 THE TYCOON WHO HEALED
HER HEART**
Melissa James

**#4290 WHO WANTS TO MARRY A
MILLIONAIRE?**
Nicola Marsh

You can find more information on upcoming Harlequin® titles,
free excerpts and more at www.HarlequinInsideRomance.com.

HRCNM1211

REQUEST YOUR FREE BOOKS!
2 FREE NOVELS PLUS 2 FREE GIFTS!

Harlequin

Romance

From the Heart, For the Heart

YES! Please send me 2 FREE Harlequin® Romance novels and my 2 FREE gifts (gifts are worth about $10). After receiving them, if I don't wish to receive any more books, I can return the shipping statement marked "cancel". If I don't cancel, I will receive 6 brand-new novels every month and be billed just $4.09 per book in the U.S. or $4.49 per book in Canada. That's a savings of at least 14% off the cover price! It's quite a bargain! Shipping and handling is just 50¢ per book in the U.S. and 75¢ per book in Canada.* I understand that accepting the 2 free books and gifts places me under no obligation to buy anything. I can always return a shipment and cancel at any time. Even if I never buy another book, the two free books and gifts are mine to keep forever.

116/316 HDN FESE

Name	(PLEASE PRINT)	
Address		Apt. #
City	State/Prov.	Zip/Postal Code

Signature (if under 18, a parent or guardian must sign)

Mail to the Reader Service:
IN U.S.A.: P.O. Box 1867, Buffalo, NY 14240-1867
IN CANADA: P.O. Box 609, Fort Erie, Ontario L2A 5X3

Not valid for current subscribers to Harlequin Romance books.

**Are you a subscriber to Harlequin Romance books
and want to receive the larger-print edition?
Call 1-800-873-8635 or visit www.ReaderService.com.**

* Terms and prices subject to change without notice. Prices do not include applicable taxes. Sales tax applicable in N.Y. Canadian residents will be charged applicable taxes. Offer not valid in Quebec. This offer is limited to one order per household. All orders subject to credit approval. Credit or debit balances in a customer's account(s) may be offset by any other outstanding balance owed by or to the customer. Please allow 4 to 6 weeks for delivery. Offer available while quantities last.

Your Privacy—The Reader Service is committed to protecting your privacy. Our Privacy Policy is available online at www.ReaderService.com or upon request from the Reader Service.

We make a portion of our mailing list available to reputable third parties that offer products we believe may interest you. If you prefer that we not exchange your name with third parties, or if you wish to clarify or modify your communication preferences, please visit us at www.ReaderService.com/consumerschoice or write to us at Reader Service Preference Service, P.O. Box 9062, Buffalo, NY 14269. Include your complete name and address.

HR11B

USA TODAY bestselling author

Penny Jordan

brings you her newest romance

PASSION
AND THE PRINCE

Prince Marco di Lucchesi can't hide his proud
disdain for fiery English rose Lily Wrightington—
or his attraction to her! While touring the palazzos
of northern Italy, the atmosphere heats up...until
shadows from Lily's past come out....

*Can Marco keep his passion under wraps
enough to protect her, or will it unleash itself, too?*

Find out in January 2012!

"**B**rittany?" His voice was deep and pleasant and made her realize she'd been staring at him openmouthed through the screen door.

"Yes, I'm Brittany and you must be…" Her mind suddenly went blank.

"Alex. Alex Crawford, Chad's friend. You called him about a deck?"

As she unlocked the screen, she realized she wasn't quite ready yet to allow a stranger inside, especially a male stranger.

"Yes, I did. It's nice to meet you, Alex. Let's walk around back and I'll show you what I have in mind," she said. She frowned as she realized there was no car in her driveway. "Did you walk here?" she asked.

His eyes were a warm blue that stood out against his tanned face and was complemented by his slightly shaggy dark hair. "I live three doors up." He pointed up the street to the Walker home that had been on the market for a while.

"How long have you lived there?"

"I moved in about six weeks ago," he replied as they

walked around the side of the house.

That explained why she didn't know the Walkers had moved out and Mr. Hard Body had moved in. Six weeks ago she'd still been living at her brother Benjamin's house trying to heal from the trauma she'd lived through.

As they reached the backyard she motioned toward the broken brick patio just outside the back door. "What I'd like is a wooden deck big enough to hold a barbecue pit and an umbrella table and, of course, lots of people."

He nodded and pulled a tape measure from his tool belt. "An outdoor entertainment area," he said.

"Exactly," she replied and watched as he began to walk the site. The last thing Brittany had wanted to think about over the past eight months of her life was men. But looking at Alex Crawford definitely gave her a slight flutter of pure feminine pleasure.

Will Brittany be able to heal in the arms of Alex,
her hotter-than-sin handyman...or will a second
psychopath silence her forever? Find out in
TOOL BELT DEFENDER
Available January 2012
from Harlequin® Romantic Suspense
wherever books are sold.

SPECIAL EDITION

Life, Love and Family

Karen Templeton
introduces

The FORTUNES *of* TEXAS: Whirlwind Romance

When a tornado destroys Red Rock, Texas,
Christina Hastings finds herself trapped in the
rubble with telecommunications heir
Scott Fortune. He's handsome, smart and
everything Christina has learned to guard herself
against. As they await rescue, an unlikely attraction
forms between the two and Scott soon finds
himself wanting to know about this mysterious
beauty. But can he catch Christina before she runs
away from her true feelings?

FORTUNE'S CINDERELLA

Available December 27th wherever books are sold!

www.Harlequin.com

SSE65643